Diana,

Best Wishes!

To a future of surprises and unsolved mysteries,

[signature]

Eternal Discontent

Timothy W. Phillips

Copyright © 2008 by Timothy W. Phillips

ISBN 0-7414-4513-1

Published by:

INFI∞ITY
PUBLISHING.COM

1094 New DeHaven Street, Suite 100
West Conshohocken, PA 19428-2713
Info@buybooksontheweb.com
www.buybooksontheweb.com
Toll-free (877) BUY BOOK
Local Phone (610) 941-9999
Fax (610) 941-9959

Printed in the United States of America

Printed on Recycled Paper

Published July 2008

Preface

One hundred years from now, we will see something happen that, in the history of our great country, we have never seen. Some of us may have dreamed that this would eventually happen, and others may have discussed such an event with friends at the occasional social gathering. Yet, fortunately, none of us will live to see what has been foreseen. So, when I say "we will see something" I am speaking of this once powerful, already failing to progress, nation which the world tends to both fear and hate. Do I wish to be alive to experience it? A little piece of me wants to be. It wants to be able to experience the thrill of change as it evolves our everyday lives. On the other hand, at my age, I am afraid I would not be able to handle the changes we will have to face. I fear I will not be able to adjust to the sacrifices expected of us.

How do I know this will happen? I have seen it. I have envisioned the events to come. Don't think I am crazy, as the others do. I *can* see the future. Some have called me a psychic or have given me names such as Oracle or Philosopher. Others see me as a freak of nature and fear to hear my words. Do they shove me aside and dismiss my words because of how I look? No! My bewildered homeless aging appearance does not intimidate them. Unfortunately, they fear the reality of what I can see. You are probably asking yourself, "Will these events really happen?" I believe so. I believe I have been sent here to warn you of events to come. I am not here to scare you or bring false stories of the future. Telling lies about dreadful events is not how I wish to live out the remainder of my days. Bringing persecution upon myself, for no logical reason, makes no sense. I am simply here to tell my tale and educate you about what is to come. What you choose to do with my words is up to you. My story will save you, or, at the very least prepare you for what awaits.

When it happens, we won't know who is left on our side. Our families will be torn apart. Communication with loved ones will be forbidden! They will be dubbed outcasts. Even worse yet, our families will be unrepentant as they meet their death. They will be viciously slaughtered by the system and its unstoppable ignorance. Our minds will become illegal tools, thought to be used against the "government." Or at least, that is what will be said. Free will and freedom of choice will become discouraged ideals recorded in history books. You will no longer be able to openly voice your opinion. If you do, it will certainly be the last time. Your friends will be your enemies, and your past enemies, your newest friends. It will be as if two new races of human beings have molded new societies carefully guarded from each other. One group will consist of those found on the higher rungs of the governmental hierarchy. The other will be made up of those who fight desperately to hold onto those things lost.

What would it be like to have your every move monitored by those in power? Who could stop them from doing this? You do realize that it is already beginning. No? Who is watching when you log on to the net? Who is listening when you make that phone call? Already technology allows them to spot you through satellite and pinpoint your exact location. Give them one hundred years and the farthest fetched science fiction will become scientific fact.

The world currently operates on its own, oblivious to the forces changing their lives. Never stopping to look at the hidden agenda driving society. When will it be too late for you? When will you finally realize the dangers eating away at your freedom?

While these events have already been put into motion, the main incident of chaos will happen nearly one hundred years from now. What exactly is going to happen? Everyone wants to know, but nobody cares to believe. Curiosity makes the soul desperate. Our society, our way of life, is going to change dramatically. Ah, I have tiptoed around the answer long enough. We will see The War! Yes we've seen war before, but this is going to be the one that fills our minds with doubt and fear. Many of you already believe you have seen it. But it has not yet come. You will see!

When the war is realized, no one will want to be a part of it, and practically nobody will be a direct participant. Most of the world will be forced to sit back and watch as the fighting changes their existence. Can we prevent what is going to come? We cannot! It is not our choice! We can't control destiny! We cannot stop its momentum! A diluted few will try, but it will be too late. Destiny will put us in our situation, and I am sorry to say there won't be any person capable of preventing it.

Madaggan... Remember the name. He will be strong-willed and bull-headed. Through persistence and hard work, he will come to be a well-loved and respected man of this great country. He will rise up through the government quickly, and he will be seen as a hero above all others. But even as I advise you, I already know society will either ignore or forget my warning. Perhaps if I describe more of the future you will not be so quick to dismiss my words.

A president will be elected, but he will not deserve to be in office. The people will want him removed, and this will initiate Madaggan's actions. He will kill the leader and become our new president. The people will believe this to be a positive change for their country. Americans will support and adore their murderous leader. They will be shockingly and easily swayed. Not one citizen will question what he has done nor will they worry about what he is going to do. The country will be convinced Madaggan will solve the country's problems.

In his first year, he will restructure what the government can do for and to the people. This will appear to be well-meaning. As Commander-in-Chief he will use the military to police the country. It is necessary to say that local and state police will become irrelevant... unnecessary. Madaggan, however, will think to the contrary. He will use them to protect his own cause. Any law enforcement personnel, who dare stand in his way, will be eliminated. He will easily recognize who supports him and who does not. Sacrifices will have to be made. This man will deceive those who have aided him in obtaining his goals. His madness will create a force not to be disputed. Capitol punishment will be reinstated for the entire country. Oppose him and he will be rid of you by sending his henchmen. All that we have done to make this country free will be sent on a backward spiral.

His measures for war are extreme. He believes, as all Americans egotistically believe, that we are unable to be defeated. We have and will underestimate the world. The rest of the world will stand by and watch us fall under the control of this maniac. He will be the one to press the button. He will be the one to send the nukes! He will start The War! This catastrophe will be known as Madaggan's War. It will shatter, scatter, and destroy all of America. It is unavoidable! It is unbeatable! No one can prevent it!

These are my words and no one else's. Believe in them if you wish. I don't mean to scare anyone. That was never my intention. Nor did I intend to lead anybody astray from what they think will come to be of this great country. I simply present myself as an informer. Yet, my heart aches, for I know none of this will matter. By the time everything is set in motion there will be none who have heard or seen this. Those who have seen it won't believe it until it has already happened. If you do happen to see the story written before you, then remember this one thing I have not yet mentioned. This event will create a new nation and this new nation will be led by another man who knows nothing of his value to the people.

Will he stand as a true leader? Will he know why he stands or what he stands for? He will struggle with the odds piled against him and not be able to save the future.

Good luck to those of you who fight for your cause and good riddance to those of you who do not believe in a cause.

I

A well-respected man leans against the cement wall of his unfinished basement. Some know him as Chuck, others Bob, and a few call him Phil. One boy calls him Grandpa. His name means nothing to him. No one truly knows his birth name, nor is it necessary to survive in today's world. That name faded away when the war began, and the government decided that he would be a number. Fake names are used as a way of simply greeting fellow under grounders, people who have left the Zones and managed to successfully infiltrate the system. Though they lack names, all of the under grounders are linked by a common cause.

Nights like tonight serve as a calling to bring together supporters of that cause. They meet so that they might link the past with the future and sort out the process through which the zones will come together and overthrow a repressive government. A select few of tonight's older members remember when the government supported the rights of the minority opinion over the aggression of the majority's ignorance. Now, there are only those who live life free of restrictions and controls and those who have temporarily adapted their lives waiting for the day of revolution.

At the age of fifty-five, Grandpa studies the room of faces interacting quietly with each other. The murmur of the crowd does not rise as people slowly filter into the confines of the dusty basement. An occasional pair of feet can be seen moving past the small rectangular windows at the top of the basement walls. Shadows reveal their presence to any concerned party before the body enters the front door and molds into the mingling crowd below.

Grandpa runs his fingers through his silver streaked brown hair and exhales calmly as he collects his thoughts for what he has to say to this expectant crowd. A variety of ages of men and women sit and stand before him. They wear the many different expressions of life on their faces. The young seem to be more excited and energetic, but the majority of the mass appears worn from the days of the past. Many sit impatiently waiting to hear what this original zoner has to say. After all, he is one of the reasons so many of these people have been able to make it into the *civilized* cities.

Many of these people wear grey, torn clothing, the clothes they were wearing when they first came to the city. Although some of these people hold jobs that would allow them to dress in much better attire, they prefer to resort back to and empathize with those who were left behind. They wear their torn clothing and rough knuckles in remembrance of the cause. Some of them come directly from their missions, the task of digging and scraping away at the Earth so that they can keep their goals on course.

A little boy, the six year old grandson of Chuck or Bob or Phil, sits perched on the top of a set of low shelves housing a plethora of canned goods. No one pays any attention to his fragile existence as he scans the room for new faces and children to play with. Of course, there are never any children. Children can be a threat to the cause. Just one word about this meeting and an entire family could cease to exist. Therefore, J did not expect to see any children. He knows what it is like to lose his family, as his was yanked from him just over one year ago. He doesn't truly understand why, but knows that when Grandpa has a lot of people over, he cannot talk about what he sees.

No matter how many times J hears his grandpa speak, he always finds the words intriguing. Many of the people simply smile and nod at J as they acknowledge his presence, mid-sentence talking with a fellow under grounder. J smiles back and situates himself better on top of the canned good shelves.   He waits for tonight to begin and for his grandfather's motions and the volume of his voice to mesmerize and captivate his attention.

Grandpa steps onto the small pieced together plastic stage as he readies himself to speak. When he steps behind the podium, the dull murmur that filled the basement is instantly silenced. More than fifty people have crammed their tired bodies into this tight space. Focus immediately shifts to the front and center of the room in anticipation of the words about to fill their ears.

Grandpa stretches his 5'8" body so that his average size appears more formidable than it is. He sweeps over the on looking group with his hard brown eyes. He reflects on his own rough life as he sees the mass of grey before him. Finally, he speaks to them.   His voice is powerful and commanding; his message is a seed that enters through their ears, plants itself in their thoughts, and germinates to fill not only their minds, but their souls and hearts as well.

"Through time events are ever changing, creating a new history of disorder and chaos," he pauses to add effect to his words. "As the days continue to go by, people wonder what will the next page in their book hold for them. My book shows that the past has not been easy! I have truly had my fair share of instances to make my life interesting.   I don't expect my future to hold any respite from the stresses of life. I know that there is a day, waiting to meet me that will introduce me to my end. I will cordially meet that time with no objection. I have led a full life and regret nothing of it. Shall I be doomed tomorrow, I would die knowing that I have done all I can for my people. May they know that I fought for them through and to the bitter end, as vicious as my end may come to be."

The crowd's worn appearance lightens as words spill from the orator's mouth. Some nod as he talks as if to say that they understand. Others stare with their mouths slightly agape, listening to his speech. Every few sentences a person or two interjects to loudly proclaim their agreement.

"In my time, people have learned to mistrust the system. We have developed the knowledge, which has shown us what Big Brother does not want us to see. That is, we have discovered that continuous watchful eye that seeks to control us all." Grandpa pauses and listens for reassurance from the people.

"Now, it is a time where we are better off uncivilized. The uncivilized are the only ones who have a chance right now. They possess more freedom from control than any of us have seen for decades. The uncivilized parts of the existent world, live in the past as if they were never able to modernize. They will be the ones that control the future. They know how the world worked before Madaggan's War. They have secured their chances of survival by staying away from our technologically overwhelmed world."

Most of the crowd has experienced some part of their lives in this *uncivilized* place. The absence of technology is not always true, but where it is present, it is a threat to their existence.

"This knowledge has changed the philosophies of many people. We no longer focus on the present. We look back at what has been and forward to what may, someday, be again. The future brings promise, and the past holds the key to that blessed future. Yet, we know it can never be the way it was. It can never truly be restored. Even through revolution! No one will ever be able to satisfy everyone!"

A small burst of cheering sounds out from the group. Quickly, it is turned off as Grandpa begins again.

"He is soon to come! He will deliver us! In your time, you will see what I am talking about. The system will meet many challenges from the rebels. We are already making sure of this! Each and every challenge will slowly drain the strength of the system. Each pathetic attempt by the

4

government to strike down the opposition will add a little fuel to that eternal fire of life that we so dearly possess. That fire will make us victorious!"

"Revolution!" a member cries out from the back of the masses.

"The government doesn't know who their enemy is or where we come from, but we will make ourselves and our causes known. Each cause will differ from the next, but those differences will give us strength. We will draw upon these strengths and overcome the repressive government."

Grandpa is not the only one holding this style of meeting tonight. There are several groups, across the country, speaking out about how they are going to eventually rise with the masses and shut the watchful eyes of Big Brother. It is only known that there are others out there. It will take time for their causes to connect and join together for the uprising to occur.

"No one within the arms of Big Brother's organization knows exactly who the rebels are. They have an idea of where we are from, but they cannot find us no matter how carefully they search. Legends fill our ears with tales about a force. A force that will destroy the system. Yet, when it falls, I fear we will not have the immediate victory that many of us would like to see."

"Pity them!" another rings out from the crowd.

"Chaos will have its time to reign! After the oppressive government fails, the victors will destroy themselves through their anarchy. This period will be nothing in comparison to the wait that many of us have endured under the current control of such a totalitarian society. After the confusion, then we will once again have the strength to develop our Utopia. Not like the one Thomas Moore invented, but an existence of peace and rest from worry. This will be a time when people are again governed by themselves and the majority controls policy. No more minority rule! No more cockroach rulers hiding from the people!"

"Crush them!" another hails.

"The people are oppressed, my children. They need to see the system choked upon its own policies. They want to see it fall harshly and quickly. When the people had power, the masses were much more peaceful than now. We didn't experience the suffering only once heard of in third world nations. We never knew this could happen. Never, in our wildest imaginations, have we been able to prepare ourselves for this lifestyle. Even with the occasional war, we were still capable of leading better lives than what we are currently grasping."

"Tell 'em, Chuck!"

"Of course, we had the crime and a dark perception of our own lives. We fooled ourselves into peaceful solutions by turning our heads instead of confronting what we knew was wrong. Even then, organized crime was not as dangerous as what we now face.

"As long as mankind has free will, we will have destructive habits and more. But the worst, of these moments faced, in the past, were nothing compared to what we face now. When a person acts out, it is much more catastrophic. They know they can die for simple crimes, so they go out to destroy and take themselves in the process. Strap a bomb on and go until they try to stop you! Then, when they get close, wreak havoc. Desperate fools!"

"Crazies," a couple murmurs close to the stage.

"The system used to protect us from harm. Now, it destroys and commands us, like a pack of wild dogs, with fear lingering in the depths of our minds. Wondering, every day, if the pack is going to knock down our door, corner us, and eat us. Our voices are no longer heard as we slouch in our corners. Our needs are no longer met as they destroy our lives. They used to speak about 'Life, Liberty, and the

6

Pursuit of Happiness...' These are common words, of the past, that we are no longer privileged enough to feel!"

"Tell 'em Bob!"

"Those who are rich and have enough money to control what the government thinks. They are the ones experiencing most, if not all, of the freedom from the eyes and ears of the ever so desperate 'Big Brother.' The uprising of Madaggan's administration threw out the Constitution and all of our freedoms along with it! Little did we know that we were supporting the wrong candidate to lead. Richards' ideals were supposed to make things better, but they didn't. So, with drastic results, we supported this freak."

"How wrong were we?"

"After the people rise again, you must understand we will have to start all over. We work for pitiful wages and lead pathetic lives. They consume our earnings with warfare on the common criminal who is only fighting to have a better future. Your kind cannot understand any of their reasoning. You are too young. Thought to be educated, but they keep you as uneducated as the rest of the world. They have kept you in the dark for so long." Grandpa changes his direction to those who are newer to the group.

"They will continue to keep you there. They don't even allow you to have a grasp on what is real. How can we expect to hold the hope of a better future in our hearts? We only pray that reality will break into focus and our present will fade out.

"I wish you could have seen what it was like forty years ago. Because you were not there, it is easier for you to accept the way things are today. They've taken it away from you in your innocence. They've sheltered you in ignorance and diverted you from the past. You haven't lost what we have lost. If ever you were to see those days, you would have a better grasp of our current struggles. Then, you wouldn't have to fight us and help them hold us back!"

"Respect!"

"They have had all of your lives to wash their philosophy over your minds. Every thread has been woven through in the classroom and the environment by which they surround you. From birth, they inject you with their crap!

"The social elite currently have control of everything. Yet, it is your generation who will be responsible for shutting them down. You will have to reverse everything. Unlearn what you have been taught and accept your newest fate. Your time is soon to come!" Grandpa points a finger at the crowd. His voice escalates in volume.

"When He comes, much will be changed. What your generation does during this chaotic period of time will make all of the difference. I am certain that, unfortunately, none of them are ready for this. It's getting to be too late. We have worn them down and made it even easier now than it would have been ten years ago. Your cowardly peers possess the nature for rebelling, but they haven't the reason to fight! If the reason were there, then the cause would create its own destiny! Destiny would be left leading to success and then onto better things!

"Don't get me wrong, they have a strength that not even I can understand, but that is just not enough when coming up against this government. When it comes down to it and they have their chance to change the world, will they rise to the occasion? Will they unite themselves against a common foe, or will it continue to be a black and white issue? Will they fight back to back or one at time? Their choices may destroy them! They will need to set aside their differences and find a common ground for just this one life-changing event!

"Your generation can hoot and holler, but is it really what we need? When it all happens, you will see what I am trying to say. Yet, you too, may not be ready. We only hope that we have raised you to be able to separate yourself from the crowd. Become the leader! You will need to! It is absolutely essential that you do! In the end, it's they who are ready and willing to pull themselves away from the crowd who will be successful in defeating this overpowering system! It's your choice!"

The crowd nods in unison. This is not the first time they have heard these words. Will the ages of tomorrow, lead them into the future? Or, will they fall aside and allow the government to control their actions?

"Prepare yourself for the worst! You may see it. We are either drawing closer to the end of our suffering or coming to a whole new beginning of restrictions and limits on our own lives. It depends on the revolution itself. Fight on or sit on your hands. I will not be here to see either. I am old and hated by them. They are continuously chasing me. Fortunately, they haven't yet come with the night. But, they will be here soon. If I don't die of old age, I will see the bullet of some kid's blaster. It is up to your generation.

"Be aware of the watchful eyes of our Big Brother. If they know what you have come to know, they will do whatever they have to in order to prevent you from being successful in resisting them. If they find out what we have been talking about, they will eliminate me. I am the informer. That makes you innocent... for now. When they come for me, you will have to react as if we have never had this conversation. Besides, I am the outcast to their incompetent system of oppression. Anything you hear can be erased from your memory by a short visit to their confinement labs. Or at least that is what they think. They'll drug you and continue to do so until you no longer remember why you are taking the injections or what life was like before they began. Then, they'll release you into society and expect you to function without any problems. Expect you to play their puppet.

"If ever they are after you, trust no one. They are all around us. Our brothers and sisters are against us. They even have our best friends. Who can we really trust? Even you could be a danger to me. Your parents were. The only person I have found myself able of trusting is the one who I know least. They have a chance of being the uninformed nobody who will misjudge me. On the other hand, those people closest to you already know who you are. We have to face the fact that the system knows everything about us and controls our lives with their rules. There is no justice!

"Sometimes, to sacrifice is better than to be the victor."

II

15 years later

BooM!!

A loud explosion comes from the main floor of the house shaking the walls and loosening the dust resting on the rafter above J and his grandfather. Sitting in the basement, they hadn't been able to see anything going on outside. The windows had been tinted over by age and dirt. Yet, they knew it was time. They knew this moment was approaching. They knew about the raids that Citru had for the past few months. It was only a matter of time before the Citru Police decided to attack grandfather's place.

J and Grandpa had been planning their response to this event for the past two years. They knew that whatever was to take place would end on this day. They had been studying their offensive, like a championship football team in the locker room. Grandpa and J knew what was about to happen, how to deal with it, and they were ready. The sudden explosion of a splintering wood door jolted them into the instinctive action they'd been planning out for too long now.

BooM!! BooM!!

"You know what to do, J!" Grandfather picks up his double-barreled shotgun and knocks over the table in the corner of the basement. The wooden tabletop clunks on the floor. It isn't going to be much protection, but it will have to do for now.

The stairway is the only known entryway to the basement. From here, he is praying to be hidden from any clear shots from the base of the stairs. Quickly, he pulls a shelf of canned vegetables away from the wall, grabs J's thin shirt, and shoves him through the crack. It should have ripped in protest to his grandfather's sudden jerk, but miraculously it didn't. Perhaps the strength of his shirt serves as a good omen.

J has no time to protest his actions. It would do no good to protest anyhow. He realizes that fate is now laid before them; despite whether or not he wants to go through with it. Throwing the flashlight into J's hands and stuffing a paper bag down his blue shirt, Grandfather closes the entranceway and ducks down behind the table.

Clutching his shotgun in his already nervous right hand, he waits as they finish breaking down the front door of his house. "If they would've tried the knob, they would have known that it wasn't locked," Grandfather mumbles to himself. Rarely ever does he lock it. The only people coming through it would be friends who sought to discuss plans of action to be handed down to the zones. Or, in this case, the police playing their traditionally violent game of cat and mouse. Unfortunately, this is always a one-sided game where they bring in rookie officers to destroy the perpetrator's home. After all, when the perpetrator is behind bars, if one makes it that far, it is very unlikely to ever see home again.

"Okay boys... This is the place! Team one, up stairs! Team two takes the basement! Bring me this man, dead or alive. Anyone who brings him to me alive will see an immediate promotion when we return."

"Yes, sir!" The eager, trigger-happy officers salute their commander.

Directly after they answer their commanding officer, a redundant shuffling of feet scatters throughout the house in

12

search of their target. The sound of breaking glass echoes from one room to another. Windows are smashed from the walls, and drinking glasses are needlessly flung from their homes in the cupboards. Anything these officers can lift, they will attempt to throw through the nearest wall. If there are any hiding places, they might hope to find one and maybe crush the hidden body with the blow. These people are here to complete a mission and aren't going to fail. They will tread on whatever and whomever stands in their way. If anything dares to move while they are on this rampage of destruction, it will be immediately followed by a flush of bullets. This is all a part of procedure. This is routine. Storm the house, tear it to pieces, and torch it. If they don't find the body, it will either be ashes or homeless. Purge the criminals from their homes and crush them in their retreat.

Upstairs, no one is found, but the team begins dumping fuel and preparing the house to be set to flames. Destroy, and then scorch. This is simply one of their typical police raids. The over-whelming stench of gasoline starts to spread through the air. They use most of the yellowed old books, resting on shelves, for kindling. Pages are torn from them and spread thoroughly over the five rooms on the second floor. They should burn easily. When they are doused in gas they will become the heart and rage of the inferno.

Team two guts the main floor trying to find the basement. They know there is one, somewhere, but for the life of them they can't seem to find it. The blue print that they had examined must have been wrong. The entrance at the back of the house is no longer there, and when they broke through where it should have been, they found only another brick wall. When they blew that out with a set of miniature explosive packets, they still hadn't found anything except another stone wall. How many layers could possibly exist to these walls? They pull the cupboards from their resting places and check every surface. They search for any switch or lever – no matter how cleverly concealed – that might open up a passage to the lower level.

Virtually everything in the house is removed from its original spot so that they are absolutely sure they didn't miss anything. Debris is scattered over every inch of the floors. After a complete search of the main floor, nothing has been found. Broken pieces of ceramics lie on the wooden floors surrounded by glass, chunks of the walls from the blast, and everything else they had thrown there. Maybe if one sifted through the rooms, they would find something still intact. Maybe not. Gas from the second floor begins to seep through the ceiling. It saturates the walls and drips onto the debris littering the floor. Obliteration of this home is moments away.

Both teams meet at the front entrance, where Captain Schmidt stands waiting for a report or a body. When he sees nobody with anything important in hand, he expects the worst. Yet, he knows something that they don't know as he has been standing in the doorway the entire time. Next to him is the new entrance to the basement.

"What are you doing?!" Schmidt looks at them knowing that they have not completed their mission. None of them had gone through the door to his right. The old man isn't within their grasp. They look back as dumb struck as a dog when it tilts its head as you speak trying to absorb the garble of incomprehensible words. "Why don't you have him?! Where is he?!" What else could he expect from a group of rookies rarely used for anything other than the routine mission of destruction?

"We couldn't find the basement, sir." They all step back to make sure that they are definitely out of their superior's immediate reach. It is known that the Commander will attack failing officers. Failing is not an option.

Schmidt glares at them, as they all seem to be nod-ding in agreement. He imagines them as a flock of Dodo birds standing and shaking their heads in unison as if mindlessly following the lead of the person in front of them. He half expects more from them. This assignment is one that many of these rookies have seen on several occasions. Yet, he knows he should not expect more than what they have already given. Leading these imbeciles is beginning to wear on the Commander.

"We finished off the second floor, destroyed practically everything we could get our hands on, and punctured through two cement walls on this floor. We just can't find the basement." Tell him the story, let him know the successes, and maybe he won't yell. Maybe they won't be stuck in the chambers tomorrow. Maybe they won't be stricken down in a wrath of anger. Just please him.

Failure in the force… Failing Schmidt can be dreadful. Tomorrow, they might all be sweeping the filth of Citru. Dealing with society's surplus population of druggies and street thugs is ten times more dangerous and tedious than their current assignment of wiping society clean of "revolutionaries."

"I know you are nothing but a group of inexperienced rookies wasting my time! Wasting the words I speak to you!" He pauses and examines the aftermath of the house. They were right; everything in his view has been absolutely, positively, obliterated. "All of this," he indicates the ransacked home, "and none of you were able to find the passage to a room that we know exists? I don't believe it. It's impossible! I can't understand how you people can be so incompetent!" He grabs a doorknob to his right side. The veins in his neck are protruding through their encasement of flesh as he is ravaged with anger and frustration. The passage to the basement was too obvious. "I guess we should just leave! Nobody is competent enough to find this guy!"

His face of rage turns to one of innocence. He turns the knob, pulls the door open, and leaves the room into what they were sure was an ordinary closet by the front door. "By the way, this closet is the entrance to the basement. Who would have figured?" He pauses and waits for something to happen. Each second passes by uninterrupted by even the slightest sound. The teams pause waiting to see what he is going to do next. The awkward moment moves on.

"Sir?" Roberts stepped forward. "Shouldn't we go down there and search?" No one else is stepping forward. Taking initiative seems to be one of the deeds the commander likes.

Basement

Grandfather sits patiently awaiting his fate. Today, death is certain. They should have been down here by now. Listening to the chaotic stampede of footsteps trampling his home, he begins to smell the stench of gasoline. Hearing the continuous rush of people, he isn't sure if he will be able to meet his fate conscious. He is starting to feel queasy from the fumes in the air and has to shake off the effects of the gas. As consciousness lingers, he tightens his grip on the trigger. At the very least, if he is suddenly jerked out of place, he might squeeze off a round into the unknowing victim toying with his soul. He doesn't expect it to save his life. He just wants an opportunity to take one of them out in the process. If he manages to only take one, his soul will live better in the afterlife.

Ready for his ultimate destiny, he flips his cross from the neck of his shirt and kisses it. This cross had been handed down through generations. The solid gold pendant is draped over in a white gold cloth. "God, have mercy." He slips his ancestors' treasure back under his flannel, rechecks his grip, makes sure the trigger lock is disarmed, and aims for his stairway target. He knows this stairwell is the only means of entrance. There is no other way into the basement. If they had checked the blueprints, they would find out that the old entrance had been filled in with layers of crap.

Concrete, bricks, sand bags, and whatever else could be used to fill in the new walls will be in place of the old stairwells.

"Come on, which one of you dirty bitches goes first!" He crouches lower, behind the table, so that no one will immediately see where his shots will be coming from. "Come on!" Patience is biting at his mind and he isn't sure if he will be awake when they come down. He is drifting on the edge of awareness. A fog begins to seep in on the outside of his eyes. Grandfather vigorously shakes his head to ward off sleep.

Main Level

"Well, Roberts, you have proven yourself worthy of genius thought. As good a suggestion as has come out of anyone." Looking beyond Roberts, he is now waiting for someone to volunteer their bravery. No one catches on. They all stand waiting and staring at the back of Roberts' head. "Who's first? Get your asses down there and bring him to me!"

As if they had all been shocked with a cattle prod and reminded of their duty, they immediately start rushing the open door. If they intend to venture the stairway unheard, they've failed. Sounding like a heard of buffalo, no one can miss their coming. They stumble over each other, down each and every step, the rubber butts of their guns continuously rapping and scraping at the walls of the narrow stairs. Running down, none are quite ready for what lies ahead. Little did they know about the old man waiting in the basement. They expected him to be there. They expected him to be unaware.

Bang! Chi Chink. Bang! Thud!

Two shots are fired from the old man's shotgun. The first just barely misses a shoulder. The second plows through the facemask of another. The defenseless plastic shield gives way to the tiny balls of fury. The bullet plunges backwards through the intruder's skull. The spread of the shot ricochets into the bodies of the others rushing next to him. The dead man slams against the wall, instantly drops to the floor, and tumbles down the stairs. His lifeless body lay there pouring blood onto the concrete and occasionally twitching as its nerves begin to realize that they are no longer needed. Wiping blood off of their shields, they stop in their places and squat closer to the ground. They bring their bodies closer to the stairs, hoping that they somehow will protect themselves in this way. The back of the rampage begins to flow over those who have stopped progressing. Momentum keeps them flowing forward. The pressure of the rear, forces the front to rush to the basement, and pray that they don't get hit.

When they reach the base of the stairs, they scatter to find the culprit. Some of the officers roll off the stairs onto one knee with their weapons scanning the basement. Others dive away from the steps lying on their stomachs as if they are about to crawl through a field of barbed wire. Left, right, and straight they force their bodies to flow so that the cop killer can be eliminated. They spread as fast as they can. The occasional shot clips another officer and sprays chunks of concrete.

Chi chink. Bang!

"Ah!" A third spread rips at the arm of another person. "My arm!" She doubles over and grabs her armless shoulder. She can feel the warm blood flooding from her stub. How can something so small, do so much damage? Soon, she too will be lying dead on the floor. They won't be able to get help quick enough to save her life. Yet, it won't be the wound that kills her.

Another officer yells out, "Behind the table!" They've spotted him among the scattered goods and chaos of streaming bodies.

The crew, on the floor, starts firing their weapons causing chunks of cement to rain down on the floor. The one sided crossfire is so immense that some of the support beams, fastened to the basement floors and holding up the rest of the house, are literally being ripped apart. Splinters of ancient wood are engulfing the air. Shells implode within the foundation, of the home, leaving softball-sized holes in the walls. Grandfather has himself spread out on the floor hoping that they won't aim low. Shrapnel and debris begin to bury him where he lay. He just needs a few more seconds to allow J to get to safety. Just a little more time. It's over for him. Hopefully, the kid learned something. Hopefully, he will remember his grandfather and what they are fighting for. It is their destiny.

"It's now or never," he yells out. Not necessarily talking to them, but encouraging himself to go through with the plan. The old man pulls a small ball from his flannel pocket. "Good night boys!" He rolls the ball across the floor, stands up, fires two more quick shots, and pulls the attention of the men away from his explosive. None of them had noticed.

This mini explosive has enough power within itself to be able to lift the house off its foundation and place it on the other side of the street. Enough power packed in its punch to get the job done. Its purpose is not for instant home removal, but to set off the trigger points strategically set out by J and his grandfather. It is strong enough, however, to promise more than doing what it is intended for.

With the extremity of ammunition unloading its wrath, no one sees what he has thrown. All they can see is the ricochet of bullets as they pass through his body and pelt the cement behind him. They strive to kill this man and focusing on that one thing, they don't see him laughing through his death. He may have not won this battle, but he dies certain that they will most definitely lose as well.

Even after his limp body lies on the ground, bullets are still violently flying through the air, pelting and jamming into every accessible spot possible. His little ball rolls under the stairs unnoticed. When the explosion came, there wasn't enough time for surprise. The impact was instant. If they were able to feel their skin ripping from their muscles within one hundredth of a second after the explosion, then they were unfortunate enough to feel the split second of pain before the rest of the house would leave a crater, the size of a small lake, on 5th street in the metropolis of Citru.

Besides instantly wiping out the entire crew and setting off the triggers, the gasoline on the above floors adds to the already large impact of grandfather's pocket sized creation. The house doesn't have a fraction of enough time to set itself on fire. A fire response unit will not be necessary at this house. Maybe they will arrive at some of the far reaching homes on the outer circle of the cavity left from this sudden unpredictable event. Or perhaps they will simply write this off as another loss and let the sufferers die.

It instantly combusts, and disintegrates, leaving a shockwave, that tears through the homes within a half mile radius of the explosion's vicinity. Because of the sudden impact, the city will be left fighting a fire large enough to drain Lake Erie. Fire prevention teams will be tackling this fire for days before it would go out. Hopefully, they are able to save the lives of the unknowing. That is, of course, if it is worth their time and politics don't get in the way.

Typically, this might not have even been given any attention. Fire crews are only sent out when the event at hand has an impact on the government. The people have to fend for themselves. They will have to raise their own fire protection services made up of good Samaritans carrying buckets to douse the fire. Yet, even this pathetic attempt will never allow them to save the thousands that might have been trapped under the structures of concrete and rubble coffins. In the case of this current event, even the government buildings will burn to the ground. Because this is so close to the government structures, there will be a response limited only to and specifically for them.

Only those who are hidden within the depths of the population will respond to any cries for help. Tears will be innocently shed by the people. Drops will stream as some strip away the debris covering those who may have never lifted a finger, had the roles been reversed. Despite knowing that these people may have never held an act of heroism in their souls, these people still dig. They dig to be part of something real; to know that they are a part of history. Yet, tomorrow, what is real and what has happened will be redrafted by those above them.

Big Brother would rather have it so that those who are being saved are actually dead. It gives them the fuel and unwritten permission to go on with capturing Zoners. If they can blame this on them; the common people will be more willing to turn over those who do not belong. The people who die will become martyrs to a cause. They will be martyrs aiding the government in maintaining its control of the population.

III

I know what to do. We've gone through this several times. As I go down the path, I have to flip each switch. Each and every switch has to be flipped. If I miss any, there is no hope. He dies for no reason. I lose my only family for no purpose. I have to turn back and help. NO! If I do that, it will only stall us. He won't have it. Stand up to your fears and let go of him. It is his time.

The switches are all out in plain sight, they shouldn't be hard to find. The ones, that are actually hidden, are the bombs I set myself. I should be able to find them with no problem. Just look for the places to trigger my memory. This requires very little thinking. I don't want to do this, but it's what we have to do. A lot of people are going to die, and it's all for the cause of the rebellion; should it actually be successful. They depend on this one act. This one sacrifice has to be made. Grandpa has prepped it for them. They are depending on this. This one event is supposed to be the *gate to opening our futures*. This should set everything into motion. I have to initiate! Do the right thing. Forget about Grandpa! He is already dead!

J waits in the passageway, which he has just been shoved into fighting with his emotions. The thought of shoving the bookcase open into the basement and dragging his protesting grandfather into the tunnel flickers in his mind for just a moment. But doing just that would kill everything. The dream of a better life would die with that one act.

The tunnel is dark and cool. He turns on the flashlight so that he can find the main breaker and turn on the strain of lights that had been rigged for the tunnel. He should have been able to do it without the flashlight, but he unconsciously depended upon it for its brief use. He flips the breaker and a slight hum kicks in followed by the glow of lights spread in front of him. It looks like a small landing strip for a personal aircraft. Only, it is obviously much smaller. From a hook on the wall, he grabs a light windbreaker, pulls it over his head, and fidgets through the pockets. He'll need this to protect himself from the dripping water that has found its way through the ground and into this maze. Grasping a skeleton key, he can slightly hear the rumbling of running people on the other side of the wall where his grandfather is. They're in. He could only guess where they are or what they are planning to do to him. He can't see why his grandfather couldn't just come along. Grasping the idea or the fact, that this is the last day he will ever see him, is practically impossible.

Is this the right thing to do? Are they really the enemy? J can't figure out why or how he could bring himself to go through with this. He only had his grandfather's word that this was indeed the right thing to do. This goes against all he has come to know. J has a good job, a home to live in, and is comfortable with his life. There isn't anything that he would want to change right now. He doesn't want to be the hero of any novel. Nor does he need the world to know who he is. Yet, he knows this is going to change everything. His existence is not the only one affected by this. Their actions are converting the lives of millions spread out across the uninhabited and life-worthy zones of the country.

If he is caught afterwards, he will be executed in the square. They may simply shoot him. Or, they'll take him to trial and label him as an enemy of the state, then let the people take care of him. God, don't let them do that. Being beaten until you're near death, then having your appendages ripped from their sockets, is never the dream of any heroic messenger.

The "system" has done well by him. Yet, he understands that his grandfather makes some sense. Whenever he held rallies, people came from all over the known surviving world in order to hear what he had to say. They came from places that were supposed to have been a part of the dead zones and in such masses that it was impossible to believe that they were never caught. Even though J was supposed to, he never tipped the meetings off to anyone. Something kept him loyal to Grandpa, yet unable to talk with anyone about the stories he told.

They are watching us! Our freedom has been traded for their riches, their power, and their way of life! We suffer! They continue to live and treat themselves to our unreachable dreams! All the while we simply sit back and watch! Some of us not even known! Some never to be remembered! We can't allow this to go on! Not any more! We must rebel! Grandfather was always talking about how *They* were going to use everyone to bring the rich elite, in this country, to their ultimate strength.

Generally, most of the visitors were older. Often, there wasn't ever a person less than twenty years older than J. Lately, these people began bringing their children and grandchildren with them. Some of them, J could remember from his own classes. Others weren't from the area, and he had never seen them before or after these meetings. Shockingly, none of these kids ever mentioned these meetings to their teachers or shared opinions with J after that night. Had they done so, the sessions would have never been as successful. A system built entirely on one of two things; trust or promises. Had *They* known, *They* would have come in storms to stop everything.

Every night Grandpa and J would prepare the escape route and set the plans for the destruction of half a city block. Stringing explosives through tunnels dug out by the two of them, J wasn't sure exactly why so many people had to die. He would always try to talk about it and find out a good reason. Sometimes he hoped to find another way to do it. He liked to call it moral. Grandpa called it brainwashing.

They've already flushed your brain of any clear thinking. They did this to themselves. We're just making

24

sure that the delivery is on time! It's their fate. They live for it and they will die because of it. It won't be our fault. You can't think of it that way. We have no chance, if we sit around worrying about the morals behind all of this. Do you think they cared when our families were wiped out during the war? They will bring it onto themselves. We are just setting up the traps. We are introducing them to their fate!

When he would talk to Grandfather, he never knew exactly what was going on. He knew that the man was an extremely influential person. It was like he belonged somewhere else, not conspiring to save the futures for some people that he couldn't be sure still existed. Questioning him, sometimes, wasn't worth the effort of waiting for the answer. By the time the answer came out, J would be so confused about the topic that he had forgotten what the initial question had been. He never really found the answer he had been looking for. People are going to die for nothing. That seemed to be the only real answer he could come across.

But, what if we do this and there is no one out there that will be benefited? Maybe the question had already been answered. Maybe he is too young to understand the bigger picture and all, but a heartless massacre is what they are going to perform and killing has never been his life long ambition.

Listening for the cue, J strains his ears so that he can hear what is on the other side of the wall. By now, he is beginning to be able to smell the gas that has been spread throughout the house. Feeling nauseated, he doesn't want to stand around and wait any longer. He knows that waiting just a few moments longer might make it too late. If he passes out here, the cause, whatever that may be, would die here. Hopefully Grandpa doesn't pass out on the floor. There would be no future for the resistance. There would never be a revolution. It would die along with them.

Gotta move. Without waiting around for the cue, J flips the first switch by the passage entrance. Click. Hmmmm. One of the miniature generators pumps on and begins to work. Success! Eight feet later... Click. Hmmmmm. Another switch triggered and the sound of yet another generator grinding into action. As J walks through the passageway he continues to flip the switches. Before he moves on he quickly reads a message at each switch leading him to the next generator. Box 3, 4 steps, left wall. Generator 4, 10 steps, up on the ceiling. This continues on for the next 6 triggers. Each trigger brings him closer to finishing the job. As easy as it may have seemed, to do this, the directions are written in a code that only the two of them know. They both had to memorize the code so that all of the switches could be turned on in the right order. Should anything go wrong and somebody find this tunnel, they would have never been able to set the mechanism in motion without knowing the coded signals.

At the end of the first ten switches, J crouches to the floor, removes an old wooden board covering a hole in the ground, and crawls through. He had dug this part of the path himself. It was only big enough to fit him. Had Grandfather come along, they would have split up and he would have been responsible for this part. There weren't any switches in the other path. It served as one of several funnels for aiming the blast in just the right direction. Grandfather was supposed to have doubled back and met up at the rendezvous point. That is, of course, if he would have come along. J doubts that that would have ever happened. He had planned suicide all along. He remembers Grandpa's words, *I'm getting old and my purpose hasn't yet been met. I've got to do this my way.*

Pulling a few mirrors from his jacket pocket, J wipes away any dirt covering the lasers he had placed here weeks earlier. After the dirt is cleared away, he sets a mirror on top of each laser, thus triggering even more generators. There were no lights strung through this hole, so he had to feel his way through the dimly lit crawl space. He finds his five switches, travels through the path, and heads down yet another hall. This hall is only about fifteen feet long, and there are only 3 generators. Quickly ventured and easily finished.

At the end of this hall, he looks directly above him and uncovers his second board. A sign, reading (central office) was stuck to the ceiling so that J would know exactly where he is and what he has to do next. Behind the board, a different lever is hiding. He pulls the lever and one door slides closed behind him as another opens immediately before him.

The central office is the place where Grandfather says it all happens. *This is where all of us are being watched.* J could remember some of the stories his grandfather told him, about the place, when they were working on these tunnels.

They've got these boxes in this building. In these boxes, you can find everything about anything you and I may or may not ever want to know. They are always recording what we do. They can't keep the stuff in their computers because computers are so easily hacked into nowadays. Of course it's against their order, but the system isn't strong enough to stop all of the hackers. They come in from everywhere. The government keeps the records for at least 50 years beyond the death of anybody. That is, of course, if they aren't able to positively identify whom they have eliminated. Just in case that person shows up later. Do you think they care though? He would always pause after he asked that question. He never really wanted it to be answered. On several occasions, J had made the mistake of attempting to do so. Grandpa was just setting himself up to give his own answer. The way he spilled the rest could often be mistaken as sarcasm.

No. Those damn government people would rather see us die as a mass. The more of us there are dead, the less paper work they have to do. The less of us, the less they have to worry about controlling those who they cannot. Then, you wonder about children? Our beloved government put a restriction on child bearing. No one would have ever imagined this happening to us. Yeah, China, Japan, Russia, and Canada had been enforcing these types of restrictions. Why us? They had to save the resources. Too many people were eating up the resources. After the war, they feared they wouldn't be able to access the resources needed. This fear puts too many people in a limited area depending on limited materials. One child was allowed for every family. Who would have guessed it would have come to this. You are my only grandson. When your mother had another, they killed her and your father. J never knew his parents. He hadn't been old enough to collect memories from which they could be remembered. Yet he knew them through Grandpa. He thought they had died in an accident, but Grandpa stood behind the idea that the government had them eliminated.

This was the first time he had heard his grandfather mention them. This was also the first time he had ever even tried to strain for a memory of his parents. It was also at this time that he was given his first picture of his parents, with him in it. He was too small to be able to remember them, but Grandpa was quite capable of talking about them and how they grew up together. He wondered what life would be like if they were still here. So did Grandpa. Maybe their death shook Grandpa into this frenzy of the *government is bad*. If they were here, maybe he wouldn't be doing this. Suddenly, he felt hatred bubbling up inside him, but he wasn't sure if he should hate the system for having them erased or them for abandoning him.

He would frequently pull out his picture card and flip through the holographs of his family. *Eight children we had. Eight! Those people up there.* He always pointed to the same spot. *They passed the laws allowing my children to only have one of their own. What do they think this is, Heiro?*

28

Heiro was a small island that had been so thickly inhabited that they could not feed themselves. Even their fertile island would not provide enough food. In order to solve the problem, the government forced the poor to migrate and killed those who refused to leave.

The central building will soon meet its doom, J"

J brushes some dust off of a metal box, on the wall, to the left of himself. He opens it, brushes away some cobwebs, and flips the switch. Hmmmm. The ever-familiar sound of yet another generator adds to the already echoing background of the others. "Yes, Grandpa, they will all regret ever doing wrong to you."

He is almost done. In a few minutes, there is going to be an explosion, and J does not have to be around to witness it. He had seen the test sights from the past. He knew the wrath that this type of blast had created in this country's past. Grandfather had pictures from when Madaggan had tested this. The little marble type bomb that Grandfather was going to use, on top of the mixture of liquid gasses that the invaders were known to use. Then, one has to figure in the combining effect of the generators. A massive onslaught of death is about to present itself.

Each generator is equipped with two chemicals. J has no idea what they are technically called. He never understood chemistry when he sat in class, and he rarely ever listened to the description of each chemical when Grandpa was setting that part of the bomb together. He was too busy trying to convert the damn code so that he could write out the directions. Ultimately, he knew that when they mix, they created an extreme movement of molecules and heat. The movement forces the liquid to move down a tube path, set up by Grandpa. As each generator is kicked into play, it allows for the dissolved mixture to blend in with the newer. All of them, minus the last, are worthless. One more substance, added at the end of it all, will create a nuclear substance waiting for what grandfather calls baby formula. When the switch for the formula is thrown, it takes two minutes for it to get to the final chamber in the walls. Grandfather is depending on his steel reinforced concrete walls and the surrounding earth to be able to stop any blowouts from the holes they had dug in the ground. When that last mixture gets to the final chamber, it will bring down every structure on top of it. Hopefully it will travel the tunnels exactly how they had planned.

J is ready to finish the job. He looks up the ladder to his escape. All of them have to die, and he still doesn't know why. Yet, he doesn't bother with it. It is definitely too late. Can't turn back. Can't reverse the chemicals. He climbs the ladder and unlatches the cover. He slides the cover off and looks at his final switch. No turning back now. He flips the switch, pulls himself out of the trap hole, and appears in a room full of boxes. Two minutes.

He has just stepped into the garage where J and Grandpa had been saving everything for the mission. The digging utensils, tubing, empty chemical barrels, and a few extra generators were hidden under some empty boxes. After the bomb goes off, there won't be anything left for evidence. Even if they find any, it will be useless to try and do anything with it.

Scraping through the rubble will show fruitless re-sults. Finding evidence, to convict someone with, means actually having to do some real work. Real work takes time. Time is something the government does not want to spend on something they consider as worthless. So, they go the quick way. Plant evidence, and convict someone who may be innocent. To them, all people are guilty at one point or another. They are all an enemy. Even if they've worked successfully in federal buildings for over thirty years, they are still the enemy.

Buried under the boxes, the escape vehicle sits wait-ing for J to activate. It looks like a cross between a small car and a space capsule. In this period, some fun transportation tools have been developed. There is no longer a dependency upon gasoline. Scientists have been able to create a combustible fuel, which can be maintained through small 12-ounce alloy containers. This small cell contains enough power to run this particular vehicle for at least three months. Not only is it economically efficient, it is also strong enough to fuel every type of vehicle at whatever performance level that pod needs to maintain. Of course, the length of time that can be drawn from the fuel cell varies according to size and performance expectations. This particular Dupod is going to be able to out run any resistance. Consequently, it will burn an extensive amount of fuel, and the cell won't last the typical 3-month length.

With unmatchable speed, the balance of a legendary cheetah (before extinction), and a center of gravity closer to the ground than dirt itself, a person is strategically capable of navigating himself and one other person in this vehicle. Lying on your back, everything is controlled through two glove-type steering mechanisms that fit over a person's hands. One can consistently manipulate the viewing screen and give oneself the ability of having the machine practically drive itself. If needed, there is also a way to handle the pod through the use of the gloves. Pulling slightly with one's fingers, means turning the dupod quickly around any corner. It has the ability of turning in a complete 180-degree spin and shooting off in the other direction within a matter of a few seconds without any time or hesitation spared. Currently, this is the most agile machine on the market. Of course, it has been manipulated so that it would be capable of these complex maneuvers. Nothing and nobody will catch him. At least that is what he has been led to expect.

J hops into the dupod knowing that he has less than two minutes before he will be toast in a heap of rubble. Turning on the screen, he runs a quick scan of this machine's abilities, just to make sure that it will be ready for whatever lies ahead. The glass door overhead closes, tints itself a dark orange to match the color of the vehicle, and presents another screen, filled with small squares, for J to navigate.

In front of him stands the door to the garage. This door is different than the typical garage door. It's a hologram that no one can see through. Hologram technology has progressed so well that it can either be a solid or a gas. In this case, it is a solid. Even though it can be seen as a solid, this does not mean that a person could build an actual structure using holograms. Yes, it can be like a shield not allowing anyone to come in, but it cannot be stacked on top of another hologram and used as a building.

Yet, if it were in its gas form, too many people would be able to see what is in the garage. That can't be allowed. J presses the hologram button, the door crystallizes, and J can see people busy with their day-to-day routines.

Now, he can go through, as could anyone else. Knowing this, he watches the screen, looking for the appearance of any other vehicles or people. Seeing that the path is clear, he speeds out of the garage. Not much time can be lost here. Pulling through the hologram, it completely disappears and reappears solidifying itself, as he is clear of the projectors. He just misses a head on collision with a GVX (garbage vehicle extractor). In response, he checks his gauges again. Maybe he missed something else. Where the hell had that thing come from?

Quickly accelerating the dupod, he zigzags through traffic with one goal in mind. Get out of the city as soon as possible. Turning right up the next street, he is heading north on 5th Street. It's packed with squad cars facing his grandfather's place. As far as he can tell, no one is in them. Hopefully, his eyes aren't lying. If anybody sees him, he will be chased and arrested. The last thing he needs, right now, is to engage himself in a confrontation with the authorities.

When the police have an area blocked off, one has to stay off that part of the street. One has to pretend that there is a force-field type perimeter set up around the vehicles and surrounding area. If you go through this perimeter, you are automatically putting yourself at risk of being chased down by the police. J is going to go through them. He has to. This is the only way he can get out of town fast enough. Almost as soon as he had seen the vehicles, he passes by them. Wasting time would prove to be one of the biggest mistakes he has ever made. If he gets caught, everything has been done for nothing. All of their hard work, wasted.

Turning left onto a dirt road one mile from his grand-father's place, he crosses a small bridge over and onto an island with a higher elevation than the city. Something is telling him he has to watch what is about to unfold. Even though he was told to leave Citru and find his uncle in Pine. On the other hand, he is technically out of Citru. The island is shared between Citru and Provinctia. Ten minutes later, J is sitting on his dupod, looking through his sunglasses with binocular–like functions, and watching the action below. Eight minutes ago, the house was supposed to turn to dust. He can see the house perfectly as it sits there mocking him. People, on the streets are rushing past the house, just as he had done in the dupod. He can see them standing by the front door. They are still moving around frantically searching for the door. "They haven't found the basement, yet!"

For everything to work, that door has to be open. That door is the vent. It is one of many complex triggers set for this operation to work. Most of all, it is set to help the built up pressure travel the right path. Without them unlocking that trigger, Grandfather will simply pass out and die in the basement. The rest of the bomb will become a dud. That is, until someone opens the door.

Wondering what is going to happen, he looks at his watch and notes to himself that it will all go down within a matter of seconds. It has to. Destiny has led him this far. The thought of his grandfather lying on the floor, passed out from the gas fumes, floats through his mind. He is trying to trace the reaction of the chemicals to each other, through his head. He can envision the build up of pressure, the walls giving in under the explosion, and buildings sinking beneath the surface like Atlantis into the ocean. It will be a beautiful sight to see. "Open the damn door." Yet, so many would be crushed under the weight of steel and concrete. This would be an attack on the government that had not seen this scale of violence since the beginning of Madaggan's War. Yet it is only the beginning of the events to come.

A sudden burst of movement in the house stirs him from his thoughts. They must have finally found the door to the basement. There isn't much time now. They'll storm the basement and Grandpa will set off the final attack.

He crawls back into his dupod so that he can be sheltered from any debris that might make it this far out. There shouldn't be much, if any at all. It should all sink. That is, if everything collapses as planned. He wasn't an engineer, so couldn't really say what would happen.

Closing the hatch, he turns on the monitor and waits. To his right, where the passenger seat lay, he flips up the seat, turns on another screen, taps a few revealed buttons, and a transparent screen appears displaying the local news. He knows this event will be crawling with media. He is shocked to find that nothing has been reported yet. Not even the fluster of people in front of the house has been trapped on the waves.

Typically, when there is a big bust of someone demonizing the system, the news is allowed to break in for coverage. That is after the event is, precisely, so far into play. Throughout the city, a string of cameras had been set so that the government could keep an eye on the people and the media an eye on the government. It makes the people feel better about being 'protected.' The corporate businesses pitched in and helped to structure the program by setting up the eyes of the system. Then, broadcasting companies bought certain restricted rights to the access of these cameras. They maintain a continuous running file for shots that are allowed under their contract with each city council. Much of the live feed, shown to the city, through this film, will be used as evidence to crimes. This feed would usually be filtered before the network could touch it. A little bit of camera magic can turn any good day into a horrific event for some unknowing citizen by trapping them into whatever plot the politicians want the people to believe. Yet, it is often viewed as the actual event. That's what they want you to believe.

When the screen kicks in, there isn't anything out of the ordinary. The President is scratching himself in front of his mirror wearing his purple bathrobe and boxer shorts. It's one of those shows marketed for the country to see their leader as an average everyday person. They are continuously shooting footage of him and his family. This way the people can imitate the image of the President. Besides, he is a president for the people.

When the traditional powers of the President were eliminated, as a result of Madaggan's follies, the position became a joke. Allowing another to stand in the place of a person, with so much power, has become almost non-existent. Now, he is simply a role model for the American people. Still elected by the people, he is only a symbol of our government.

J looks at his watch one more time. Minutes have passed by. Nothing has happened. He looks at the house on his screen. Nothing. Space moves on and nothing has changed. The air is silent and empty, teasing him to run back to the house and make the desperate attempt to save Grandpa. Nothing is moving anywhere. The world continues to spin, but time seems to be frozen.

Back tracking his thoughts and actions of the day, J is trying to find out what he has done wrong. Did he miss anything? He retraces the attachment of the tubes. He listens to the sounds of the generators kicking on with the click of each chamber opening to release whichever chemical it possessed. He redid the final switch. Everything had worked out just right. The door has opened and more than enough time has gone by for the bomb to go off. He hadn't skipped or missed anything. It wasn't possible. He practiced this run everyday. He knew each step of the way. To dummy proof the network, he even wrote out directions of what to do at each switch. How far he had to go for the next one and where it was. Fool proof...

J climbs out of the dupod again. Flipping up the driver's seat so that the floor of the vehicle is presented, he reaches for the plans that lay out the entire pathway for this homemade bomb. He looks them over, checking every step off as he crosses it mentally within his mind. Each time, he recalls a picture of him initiating each step. Finishing the examination, he rips the blueprints in to small squares, stuffs them into a close by garbage shredding unit, and lights it on fire by throwing a fire stick into it. Can't keep the evidence. He was supposed to burn them at his uncle's cabin, but keeping them that long could prove to be fatal to the success of his mission.

"Why isn't this working? Damn it! I know we put it all together to the tee! Grandpa will die for nothing!" J didn't know what he should do from here. He wants to go back to the house and pull Grandpa from the basement. They couldn't have failed. It was all planned out to perfection.

IV

Captain James, a respectably older man, grins as he spins around in his well-padded leather office chair. It squeaks and scrunches under his weight as he shifts his body to a more erect position. In his hands, he holds a picture of his deceased wife and daughter. A few moments ago, he had been gently caressing the photograph, but now he looks up from their faces and stares at the boy who had just entered his office moments ago. Age hasn't begun to take hold of anything in this man's appearance. Captain James is as fit as a 30-year old man who goes to the gym every morning before tirelessly waltzing into work. For the past 20 years, he has done exactly that. Picking up his half full glass of orange juice, after setting the portrait on his desk, he takes a sip of his orange juice and grunts at the young man. Breaking his routine wasn't ever something that he welcomed with ease. Interrupting the Captain's daily routine is exactly what this young man is doing at this precise moment.

"What do you want boy?" Agitation rings in his voice. "You've been in here long enough. Speak up and tell me what it is that I can do for you!"

"Sir, I have a report, on the events on 5th Street." He pauses and hands the package to the Captain. His hands are shaking and his nerves on their ends. He knows that breaking up the officer's morning is never an easy job. Sometimes it results in negative consequences. Consequences that the young man isn't interested in seeing. Ever. Sweat beads at his hairline. James receives the package, pulls out the holographic sheet, and reads.

> At 08:00 hours, we began to stage our attack on the home, located at 36001 5th Street. Despite a few minor set backs, we have been able to freely trek through both the main and the second story levels of the home. The

37

main entrance to the basement has been relocated. Currently, we are working on finding this passage. It seems that they knew we were going to hit them soon. They have prepared themselves for us. We are positive that we will, once again, become triumphant. If you could make it here, we would enjoy your company. We understand that you are personally looking for this man. Please come and let us present him to you, sir.

"Sir, our forces are about to take out one of the biggest enemies of the state." He straightens himself out and allows the Captain time to read on. He has already interfered once this morning, irritating James wouldn't be a way to begin the day. "As you can see, sir, we are in the house right now, and we are just moments from wiping out the opposition." Yet again, he states another obvious conclusion. Nothing the Captain did not already know.

"I see." He stares at the boy waiting for him to say more. They always have more to say. They always need some sort of direction. Can't bring them to thinking on their own anymore.

"Sir, what do you want us to do?"

"Finish the job! Give the press no reason to breathe down our necks. I have already ordered for all of the accessible cameras to be turned off. They shouldn't be able to see anything. Nor should they know that any of this is going on. In two hours, we will send over a live wire to them so that they can have our version of the story. Proceed as we would with any other event of such importance."

"Yes, sir, I understand." He salutes James, turns, and walks away.

"Smith, I hope your death is fast. You won't escape this time." He pushes the page button on his desk phone: a console of buttons built into the top of the desk that works just as any speakerphone would. "Jane, I am going out, I'll be back in a few hours."

"Yes, Mr. James. I'll hold all calls."

Captain James gets out of his chair and walks to the door at the back of his office. Through this door is his own personal garage with an XTR3 sitting there waiting. An XTR3 is a standard Police vehicle that can convert from land to air to sea. Being that his office is on the 10th floor, he needs a mode for a quick escape. Attacks on officers are not common, but they are an occasional event. Because of the rare attack on officers and the fact that most vehicles are capable of flying, James was issued his own XTR3 and 10th floor garage attached to his office. If the building were to be attacked, he could easily escape.

Being an anti-gravity vehicle, it can float through the skies of the city, swerve around buildings, and speed down heavily populated streets easier than any other vehicle of its class. Of course, civilians don't have access to this model. But they can purchase similar but weaker versions of this machine.

The Captain's XTR3 is quick, but it takes time to build up its speed. Once it gets rolling, it is even harder to stop. Because of this, it is often used as a ramming device for places where debris may be blocking a road. Or when protestors need to be scared away from a picket. Despite its slow acceleration and stopping, it can quickly shift from land to air to sea. These convertible qualities make it an even better device than one might think. One could say that this is his toy. His pride and joy. With this sitting in his garage, he feels safer than the rest of the world.

He opens the large side door of the XTR3, he gets in, and it starts by itself. "Good afternoon, Captain."

"Good day, Marcy." The XTR3 is equipped to know who is in and around the vehicle, an identity tool. This allows it to almost be theft proof. There are only a few accounts of the lesser strength XTR3s being stolen. For James, the vehicle often tells him when a warrant has been issued for someone passing the vehicle. This makes for easy arrest and peace keeping. Another great feature is that it can either be driven or do the driving. Yet, of course, most vehicles now have that capability. Although he knows this, he is still extremely fascinated with the idea of having the choice of hands free driving.

"Where are we going today?"

"To the old Smith house on 5th Street."

"Directions received and you will arrive at your destination in about 15 minutes." A preprogrammed map of the home displays itself on the wall to his left. Being able to carry a miniature SWAT team, the XTR3 has a central cavity set up to show a team what their mission is and to allow them to go over tactical strategies as they are traveling to their destination. The XTR3 lifts itself from its resting place in the 10th floor garage and levitates through the opening in the wall.

Captain James turns on another holographic screen to watch the news and dims out the map. "Today, in the district of Uni, people are outraged to see that their State Representative, Paul Bartlowski, has not been present for some time now. He hasn't been in Uni for 6 months. Being a citizen of Uni, I am outraged and believe that he is not representing us to the fullest of his power. Officials believe he is on vacation, but the people are demanding that he be present. Is this but another governmental scam? Another shot at our ruling class? I mean, come on Tammy." As soon as he says her name, a group of armed officers burst onto the set.

"Bob, you are out of service." One of the militants fires at the newscaster. He drops off his chair and thuds onto the floor.

"Tammy Shant here. I don't know about Bob, but I am thankful for our security. They are doing a great job of keeping negative propaganda off the airwaves. Thank you, sirs. I thought he might attack me next." She scoots her seat away from the side of the desk and reshuffles her papers.

The security officers quietly leave the screen. "Serves them right, Marcy. We can't afford to have anyone speaking out like that. It prevents us from being able to do our jobs more efficiently. After all, who keeps the outcasts away from putting all of our lives into danger? Would we be able to effectively do our jobs, if we allowed every crook to speak out about how they think the system should be run? The system isn't run the way it used to be 50 years ago, Marcy."

"Elsewhere in the country... The President is joining relief efforts on the West Coast. Last week's storm has left hundreds of thousands of people without homes. Record breaking rainfall and mudslides have put some of the richest families into the poor house. The President has declared this area a disaster space and granted immediate aid to the area. Troops are on their way to relieve the stranded families, as we speak. Good job, sir." Tammy smiles, raises her hand to her forehead, and salutes the President. In the background, music to the national anthem begins playing.

"We need more people like her, Marcy. It would make our jobs so much easier. Instead of fighting the war so close to home, we would be able to pay more attention to the outside aggressors."

"I agree, sir."

"It's good to see that there are still people out there that support President Juan. He is so good to his people. I just wish we didn't have to continue to watch them so closely. We do have some loyalists, but not as many anymore. The illegals seem to be taking over. Are we ever going to be able to suppress them? We aren't even fully capable of keeping them out of the city."

"Mike with the forecast. Today is looking a little odd in the sky. What do we have, Mike?"

"We have enormous storm clouds rolling in from the West. Looks like there isn't anything out there to break it

41

up. So, this storm is definitely going to reach us. It shouldn't do any major damage, but I can guarantee that we will be getting poured on. There will be a little bit of thunder hitting us within the next few hours. It's nothing comparatively. We need this rain for the sake of a good winter. God knows we need this harvest. With a shortage of fertile lands, farmers are having a hard time harvesting good crops. This rain should help you guys out a lot. Back to you, Miss Shant."

"Thanks, Mike. Forecast is rain." She smiles, placing her attention directly onto the camera again. "So, if you don't have your weather suits on, you're gonna get a little wet."

Down below, life goes on. Captain James observes the many people and vehicles wandering about their own lives. Some of them not aware of the sources they cannot see. Looking on, from behind hidden spaces, cameras are watching and recording their every action. Others live knowing too much about the conspiracy of the government to control their every waking moment. Or, at least, believing that there is one. Bums still lie on the curbs of the streets waiting to get some form of handout so that they might live another day. Some of them are just as much a part of the conspiracy as anybody else might be. James figures many of them know about the underground networks bringing the illegals into the city. Unfortunately, even specially trained undercover agents haven't been able to discover all of the secrets of that world.

Yet, there are others who are rushing to their home or work ignoring everything else around them. They are ignorant to a life outside of their own. They could care less about the world outside of themselves. Because of this, they don't believe there is anybody living beyond the city. Therefore, they don't and may never help prevent them from entering it. Maybe more worthless to society than the bums whom society fears.

"Sir, I hate to break up the silence of our trip, but we are 5 minutes from our destination, and I've spotted something you may want to see."

"What is it, Marcy?"

"The orange dupod, sir."

"Really?" He rubs his chin and grins. "So the kid is on the run, huh?" The only orange one of its design belongs to J, Smith's grandson. It's not that J is suspect to anything, but he is related to the man believed to be a danger to society. He has to know something. He has to be aware of his grandfather's faults, his secret societies.

"He doesn't seem to be in a hurry. He is almost directly below us."

"Okay. Marcy, change course and follow him."

"Yes, sir."

The XTR3 rises higher to create more of a distance between the dupod and itself. Its acceleration increased in order to match the speed of the dupod. Being able to match its top speed will be impossible. It is unnecessary to have to do this, when their presence is unknown. They continue to follow past the old man's home, all of the police vehicles (an arrestable offense), and across the bridge. As they reach the island, across the river from Smith's home, James orders Marcy to slow pace and park out of sight. He doesn't want to be spotted. He isn't sure what J is up to, but he has a hunch that if he arrests him for violating police space, he will miss something more important. He watches J get out of the dupod, look in the direction of his grandfather's home, and continuously look at his watch.

"Marcy, I don't know what is going on here, but I think I am going to need assistance. Call the Westville Station and have them ready to come here. Try to make contact with the officers in the Smith home and have them be aware. Something is going down on this stormy day."

Marcy went about her business, called the station, tried to contact the others, but couldn't reach anyone, and waited for the next order. Oddly, not even their communication bands could be contacted. As time passes, she consistently retries the other officers, but continues to receive static in response. James watches J get into the dupod, crawl back out, pull out a roll of paper, write on it, and then rip it up. "Are you getting all of this, Marcy?"

"Yes, sir."

He throws the scraps of paper into the garbage and sets it on fire. Yet, another minor arrestable offense. Still, James chooses to wait and see what is going to happen next.

J is talking to himself and throwing his arms in the direction of his dupod. What is he talking about? Why is he so angry? Why is he even up here? How could they have known that the bust was going down today? Everything had been kept off line and reported in secure rooms. Do we have a leak in headquarters?

Moments later, it all happens. J falls over his dupod, Captain James is temporarily blinded from the flash of light, and his backup unit doesn't make it to their location in time. The house explodes as if it were a super nova exploding and becoming a black hole. They were both shocked at what they saw. Even though J had expected this to happen, he couldn't quite solve the mystery of what held it back for so long. James knew that something was going to present itself. Yet, he would have never guessed this was coming.

In an instant, the house was no more. Buildings, as far as they could see, were collapsing like dominoes set up to run their course. One after another, crumbling like paper in the hand of a child. Tall buildings, that had been standing for almost two hundred years, were no longer there. A giant cloud of dust covers the city streets and blinds the two men from seeing anything beyond the occasional fires started from yet even more miniature explosions within the grid of streets. Rubble scatters throughout the entire city.

Before J could prepare himself to leave the scene, James and the XTR3 were serving justice to him. Immediately hovering over J and the dupod, Marcy drops a holographic electrically charged bar cage. J tries to stand up, scorching his back on the bars of the cage. Falling back to the ground, he feels himself being lifted from the ground, grass and all. He knows what is happening. Yet, it's unbelievable. He knows his fate. He had just enough time to roll over and look at the bottom of the XTR3. A red beam light, an explosion in the distance of his sight, then silence. Darkness pursues.

V

The air, heavy with silence, presses down and crowds his consciousness as J begins to wake on the stone cold floor. The floor is not only cold, but is also hard as steel. It is steel. He brushes his fingers across it to find something that he might recognize. It's flat and smooth, but not surrounding him as a wall. He reaches further and comes to another steel object. It's a bar leading up from the floor, up, and away from him as he traces its contour. There is a space from this bar to another. Then, another. These bars are what surround him. They are the walls encasing him.

He squints his eyes, not because of a light shining on him brighter than his eyes can handle, but because they have not been open for a long time. He reaches out with his other hand to find one of the other bars. He is able to grasp one and eventually finds the strength to pull himself up to the wall of bars, onto his knees, and finally to a standing position. A light breeze blows around his cage. Not enough to make him sway, but enough to cool his body from the unknown heat source flowing from below and penetrating his freedom of a thermostat.

He looks up to see if the cage is open at the top and maybe he can crawl out. It is, but the idea of crawling out escapes him as soon as he notices that there are chains holding him there. The chains are old and rusted, but often used and cleaned. The rust is slightly polished and sanded off. Each link is an inch thick and three long.

Higher than the chains, a large rod can be seen where the chain is coiled around. He studies it. Not moving, it stares back at him as if waiting for him to try and climb out. Then, when he does, it will drop him to whatever hell he is bound to meet. Plunging to the depths of his new destiny, no one will care as he screams until his skin is singed off of his skeleton.

J wonders what has brought him to this spot in his life. What has he done to be treated like a wild animal? The dimness around him gives way to no evidence of anything that he might have done. Nothing can be seen that tells him exactly where he is. A red light blinks back in his mind as the only thing he can remember. The hill, a cage, the light, and an explosion knocking him to the ground are the only pieces of evidence that he can pull into memory.

These clues, giving birth to the reminiscence of the house and his grandfather's timed fate. For a flash of a moment he wants to break down. His knees want to give out on him and his mind wants to force him into tears. Simultaneously, he is hit with the image of his grandpa, mom, and dad. All of them are dead. None of them are there to help him through this. Whatever this is. Not that he could ever remember his parents being anywhere. His eyes fill up with tears and his nose with that stuffed up feeling that follows. He doesn't cry. He sniffs it back. He has to get to his uncle's cabin. Crying, here, won't do anything for him. It will only prove that he is weaker than the rest.

A dim light silhouettes more cages against the further darkness. As his eyes adjust, he can see that other people are also in these cages. Some are sitting with their backs against the bars. Others are moving about within the confined area; pacing back and forth. J wonders where this place is. Chains are locked at the four corners of his cage, just as they are for all of the other visible cages. Not all of them are level with his. If the lights were brighter, he would be able to see down into some of the lower ones. He is sure that others would also be able to see him.

Below, a man screams out. He's not directly below, but off in the distance and closer to the ground or hell. At first, what is said is inaudible. After he yells it a few more times, J can make it out to be "Viva la Resistance!" He yells, and screams, and blares it across the open air over and over again. He cannot be seen and he is far enough away for it to sound like a mere conversation. Why would anyone continue to repeat those words in a conversation?

Why would anyone continue to scream those words in any place? Foreigners aren't allowed to speak their native tongue. Schools have rid themselves of teaching foreign languages. Rarely ever would a person be trained to speak multiple languages any more. Those people were spies. He wants to shush the voice and tell it that it is calling trouble to its side, but it wouldn't listen to him anyway. Why would anyone listen to a kid?

Fixed on the direction of 'Viva la Resistance,' a door slides open temporarily giving birth to the cells directly within the stretch of the light's power. A person walks in and the door slides shut behind him. The words get louder as if whoever is saying it needs everyone to hear it before he goes mute. A soft thump is followed by more silence. Moments later, the door opens and closes again as the person exits. The Resistance has been silenced.

Another stronger breeze blows through the cage. This time, J looks at where it is coming from. He can see the moon, shining through a small window, far away from him. It is open and distant. Even though it can be seen and the wind can be felt, the bright glow of its light does not seem to reach the inside of wherever he is. He reaches out for it. He can't grab it. The box is silhouetted against the darkness.

"Don't worry, kid. You'll be out of your nest soon. We have to work for them." A rough voice breaks the silence. It's far closer than 'Viva la Resistance!' It's startlingly closer.

J switches his stance and presses his body against the opposite wall of the cage, away from the voice. He had not come far enough to observe all of the sides of the cage. The new voice had scared him into an overly alerted state.

"Don't worry, I can't get to you. Even if I could, it wouldn't do me any good. I have to leap at least 10 feet before I can get into your cage. Then, I would have to ask myself, 'Why the hell would I want to do something like that?'" He points up at the chains of his own cage. J can just barely see his movement. "The sensors in the ceiling monitor all of our movement."

"Who are you?" He speaks out for the first time in what seems like an eternity. His throat is dry and scratchy. Talking makes him slightly dizzy. It seems to be straining what little energy he has.

"Arthur," the man replies. "I'm nobody you want to know."

"Where is this?"

"Prison."

"Prison?" He mouths the word as if not to believe them. He couldn't have been caught. How could he be in prison? He had only heard rumors about such places. It was never much of a conversation piece.

"It's one of them higher security deals. Not your average cell. You must have done somethin' big to get in here. They had you shackled like none I've ever seen. Completely restrained." Arthur moves from the back end of his cage, to the side closer to J. "I seen a lot of 'em come in here. None ever as young as you though."

Rows of lights begin to click on. Columns of energy kick into action and bring the room to life. The chains are lowered and J can see everything much more clearly. This place holds more people than J has ever seen in his life. All of them are suspended in their cages above a massively long line of deep darkness. Even though the room is now well lit, he cannot make out what might be beneath this floor. He may not really want to know. His curiosity propels thoughts through his mind.

The chambers create one large line of barred boxes, which become an aisle for the guards and prisoners to walk through. The door, at the far end of the hall, isn't as far away as it had seemed to be just moments ago. Armed men walk by. No one is talking. They are all hushed. J says nothing. It may be wise to follow the unspoken directions of others in a place like this. Even as the men walk past him, they do not look to their sides or up from where the cages have come. Like walking sculptures, they move on, unmoved.

The cages unlock and their gates swing open. A large line of people stretches the length of the hall and beyond J's sight away from the door. He steps out and stands as they are. A whistle blows loud enough for it to have come from the person standing right next to him, but when he looks all he sees is that everyone is now facing the door. He shuffles his body to do the same hoping that no one had noticed his slow reaction.

In front of him, an older man stands as stiff as the wall next to them. An orange light is blinking on the back of his neck. J reaches back and rubs his neck to see if maybe he also has one. He does not. He wonders if he will soon be given one.

"What's going on?" he whispers to the man in front. Nothing. He doesn't even budge as if he might have been tempted to answer the question. He doesn't even say 'shh' or slightly twitch his neck as if to be tempted to see who was speaking. A clapping of feet on the ground breaks the monotone silence. J straightens himself and tries to mimic the man in front of him and the man in front of that man and so on. Squinting his eyes, he can see that some of the others also have the little blinking lights in the back of their necks.

The feet stop relatively close to him. He doesn't breath. While trying to hold his posture to match that of the others, a massive hand presses down on his shoulder. He wants to drop away from it and snap the knee of the person touching him, then make like a fugitive and run for his life, but that's instinct talking. Maybe its creativity trying to work through his veins at the wrong time. In reality, doing such an ignorant thing would mean his immediate death. Even though he isn't looking, he can sense that there are others staring at the back of his head through the scope of a weapon large enough to spill his brain in a fraction of a second. Of course, that wouldn't take much.

He allows it to continue to bear down on his shoulder. For the longest time, nothing follows. He half expects them to pull up a little surgical tray and insert one of those orange blipping lights so that he can be like the rest of the prisoners. Instead, after a voice says, "He's the one", J feels himself being jerked from the line of men.

"We've been ordered to send him," another voice cuts through his consciousness.

"Prep him for the tracer." The massive hand turns J's body so that he is now facing a mountain of a man in a fine pressed suit. James is the name printed in little block letters at eye level to J. James brings himself down to eye level like J is a kindergartener and needs special attention for whatever the man might want him to hear. "You have only one choice." His breath reeks. Sewage fills the air escaping his wide mouth. One would think that a uniformed officer might have better hygiene.

J stares back into the man's mouth. Obviously knowing that the man can tell he isn't one of the robot-like men still standing like pillars on both sides of him. He almost asks what the choice is, but when he begins to think about whether or not to speak, James begins for him.

"You are going to work for us in sector six. You're going to be like a little earthworm slithering through the mud and leaving a trail of slime wherever you go." He smiles. Stained teeth penetrate the surface. "You don't know where the others are, but you have been in contact with some of them."

"Others?" He mouths the word, not realizing that he actually said it after James had.

"The rats of society. Your grandfather's pathetic revolutionaries."

Don't admit to anything. He's trying to press you for information. He thinks that by mentioning some small parts of what any crazed conspirator might know he will be able to make you talk about Grandpa. Give up something that he doesn't really know anything about and you're dead.

James grabs the boy's arm and begins half dragging half carrying him to an unspecified destination. To his left, an unblinking diversity of men begin to move forward as another whistle gives off a short bleat. None of them breaking from their forward driven glare.

It couldn't have been more than twenty feet away from where J had been standing. They turn right and begin to descend what seems to be an eternal flight of stairs. The light at the end seemed far enough off to be considered the light at the end of the tunnel. Staring down at it, J can feel his weak legs protesting each forward movement. If James wasn't still holding onto his arm, he may have slipped and beat him down the stairs without having to fulfill his choice.

Each tiring step brings them closer to that distant light. As they end the trek, the stairs open up into a room of white walls. One would have expected another large hall, lined with doors and rooms behind them. Instead, there is only one giant room. The ceiling is at least twenty feet. Near the ceiling, there are windows through which people can look into the space below. Right now, the windows are tinted dark and J can't see if anyone is observing him. The walls have been painted over in white. Not a pure white, but more of a stained white.

In the center of the room, a steel table sits waiting for its next patient. By now, J guesses that this is some sort of operating room and that they are about to put one of those blinking orange lights in the back of his neck. The table is clean and uninviting. Nobody ever wants to volunteer themselves to a scalpel when nothing is wrong with them. Around the perimeter of his obvious destiny, trays stand waiting to deal whatever tools the doctor may wish to use. Blades and hooks haunt his imagination. What if the doctor gets cut crazy? What if this is some sort of screwed up operation that he won't really make it out of?

He is led to the table and instructed to get on it. James turns away from him and extracts something small from a closet five feet away. When he turns back to J, he notices that he hasn't climbed onto the table yet. Because he had been thinking about whether or not to cooperate or the events soon to come, J had not noticed when James was lifting him from the ground and onto the slaughter slab. He couldn't resist. Even when he tried to struggle, he found that his energy had been so depleted that he was vulnerable to whatever the man wanted to do to him. Whatever it is, please don't make it painful. Nobody can stand pain, if they know it is coming.

From above, a grated rack descends upon him. Wires hang from where each line crosses over the other. At the end of each wire, J can see the possible tools about to be used on him. James straps his arms and legs down, twisting them just enough to draw a tingle of pain to his senses. Soon, all that he is feeling will be relieved. James reveals a syringe, pushes on the plastic butt of the needle, and taps the air bubbles out of the cylinder. He jams the needle into his arm and squeezes the trigger of the sedative.

Consciousness holds on for a little while. A man, dressed in white from the head up, stares down at J. He shines a bright light into his eyes, it doesn't bother him. It is a blur. Everything becomes a blur. Noises become distant and blend in with each other in the background. Everything begins to echo within itself. Then, there is nothing.

VI

Rain pours down, crashing notes of frustration onto the roof above his head. The sounds of a thousand needles continuously attack the tin shingles and attempt to break into the slightly protected room beneath. Wetness, from the water lucky enough to complete its mission of breaking through the surface, is menacingly pelting his body from above. Cracks in the ceiling show no resemblance of day or night. The barred windows are shining through a mysterious light from the darkness. It may be a light bulb shining through the darkness outside.

Where he lay, his body is motionless, but he can feel the walls around him, vibrating with bugs crawling behind the plaster covered stones. Maybe it's just a spark of paranoia. Maybe it's a childhood fear swimming through his subconscious. He could hear their insect feet pattering through the dirty tunnels of filth and debris from within the structure. Maybe it was just his conscience acting on his nightmares of being eaten from the inside out by something he cannot see. He can't tell if the walls are solid stone, or just built to look that way.

Still puzzled and worn beyond all possible alertness, he is listening for anything beyond the rain to tell him where he is. He can't hear the outside world. He can't hear the low rumble of consistent traffic passing by. He senses no rhythmic hum. He can't even recall events from anything that has happened to him recently.

Making a nearly desperate attempt to pull himself together, he quickly sits up and throws his legs to his front. His head throbbing with pain and feeling faint, he collapses back onto the hard steel he was laying on. Rubbing his eyes to get rid of the blur, shaking his head, and trying again, he uses his arms to brace himself. He grips the end of the frame and pushes off with both arms. It works. This time he is able to keep himself standing. He sways from side to side, but manages to stay erect.

The room spins. He holds his head to prevent his eyes from deceiving his next move. He takes control of them and is barely capable of shaking off double vision.

Blinking his eyes, he checks the room to see where he is. Maybe something can trigger some recollection of a story explaining his whereabouts. Water puddles lie on the floor all around. A single grimy sink hangs from the far wall. Its place in the wall is no longer supportive of its own weight. It has broken free from the wall and is supported by a single pipe. This sink is also continuously dripping onto the floor. Someone has either left the water on, or the sink has been plugged and had been left dripping long enough to overflow. It appears to be so old that people have lost all thought of paying attention to its imperfections or caring to replace anything broken.

Next to the sink, sits a toilet hole. It is just a hole in the floor for people to relieve themselves. More convenient than the typical water guzzling bowls that most homes used to have. Not as sanitary though! Yuck! Yet, even today it is illegal for homes to have the typical bowls in their homes. They consume too much water. With water levels dangerously low and rain being a rare sight, the government has put a restriction on most sources of water use. Most of the world's water has been dubbed 'contaminated' by the War.

This hole doesn't look much like anything that J would want to go by. It looks as if it hasn't been cleaned since it was installed. Few know what might be beneath the hole through the floor. With the dripping of water and the sound of rain angrily pounding above, it is hard for him to hold back any urges to pee.

Trying to flinch off the recurring blur vision and not piss himself, he is still attempting to figure out where he is. The cold rain still beats down upon him through the cracks in the ceiling, and a colony of goose bumps develops on his neck. He has to get out of this room.

Still a little dizzy, he fumbles his way over to the only visible door. Feeling around for the knob, he is completely uncertain and slightly afraid of what he might meet on the other side. A little bit of light pokes through and around the edges of this door. He finds the knob and turns it. Nothing... It is locked. Whoever was on the other side, doesn't want him in there. Is he in prison? This can't be prison. Are they watching as he continues to try and find his way out? Where could they hide cameras in this mess?

He pounds vigorously on the door and yells out for someone to answer back. Nothing. Maybe no one is on the other side. Maybe they were waiting for him to slowly die from starvation. He continues to beat on the door caging him in the coldness. A few minutes later and a couple sore hands more, he stops wondering whether or not anybody has heard him. If there were anyone, someone would have been annoyed by his actions and at least barked at him to stop. He stands back from the door, observes it in all of its entirety. This is his most recent enemy. Dumbfound, he notices that the lock is on his side of the door. Unbelievable!

"Now, who would lock someone in a room and leave it so that this person can easily leave the room in which they should be trapped? That makes no friggin sense." He flips the lock, retries the knob, and the door clicks. Now, he can only wonder if anything is going to stop him from passing through.

Slowly pushing the door open and hoping there won't suddenly be another person on the other side, he tries not to make any noise and accidentally stir the being that may be there. Hopefully, they are sleeping. Hopefully, there isn't some strung out watch dog waiting to gnaw on his femur.

56

An unnecessary precaution, considering all of the racket he had been making just a few seconds ago. His predator would have, most likely, been ready to pounce on him.

All he can remember is being on the hill, overlooking 5th Street, watching his grandfather's house, and seeing the explosion. The fate that he wished he could change. A fate he still can't see. When it hit, he could recall feeling the impact and falling over backwards. Besides these things, he isn't sure what has happened to him since or how he came to be here. He can't recognize the place. Who would keep a room like this for someone to recuperate in?

The door opens easily. It doesn't even squeak like one might expect. Brightness shines into his eyes forcing him to squint until his pupils adjust. Adjusting to the light seems to take abnormally longer than usual. It temporarily burns to open the gates of his eyes. When his eyes finally allow him to see what is in front of him, he is shocked to see how nice the room is. It is nothing like the room of filth behind him. It is as if the door opened an entirely new world to him. Coming from a dark, moist, horrid room filled with holes and water, he had expected to find the same. A place where he might be eternally trapped. A broken down home in dire need of remodeling.

On the other side, there is a fresh, relaxing, living space, with all of the modern necessities. Someone lives here, but thankfully is not here at this moment. Plush water furniture covers most of it. Water furniture replaced wood furniture shortly after Madaggan's War. Another reason water has to be preserved. This furniture is pleasantly more comfortable than the furniture of ages ago. One would think that it would wobble about as a person sat on it, but it is quite solid for people to sit in. When a person sits in it, a tiny pump sucks water out so that it can adjust to a preset desire. To keep the water from becoming filthy and a bacterial nightmare, chemicals are shot into the water every day.

Harvesting wood was a thing of the past due to the fear of radiation. One would have to venture beyond the developed cities in order to find a forest to cut down the trees. Most of the forest areas of the country had been contaminated by nuclear weaponry. A fear of contamination kept people in the 'safe zones.' Every thing changed because of that unexplainable fear. Wooden furniture had become so expensive and rare, that the government decided to outlaw its use. Trees became a luxury item. The civilized world had them as plants in their yards, but only dreamed of standing in the midst of a full fledge forest. The system complained of over harvesting of lumber and how it would be the end of the Union. The people believed in it. They allowed wood to be something that no one would use in excess. They could have replanted. They could have made it easier to access.

J walks over to the comfortable furniture and finds himself a spot to sit. He sits in a loo (modern chair) and grabs the frequency controller so that he can turn on the hologram. He could really go for an interactive session with a game in hologram.

"What am I doing?" J questions himself. "I haven't the slightest idea where I am and look at me." He feels as if he hasn't been comfortable in several months.

There isn't anyone else in the room. It is completely silent, minus the rapping of rain onto the roof. The rapping makes him want to slouch back on the loo and fall asleep again. It is definitely much warmer in this part of the building than it is in the dungeon room next door. All of these small things make it easier for J to feel comfortable and at ease.

He isn't sure to whom he is the guest, but his level of comfort is helping him to decide to take things as they flow for a while. Wait for the owner to come home. After all, they haven't harmed him yet. Besides, it's raining outside. Going out there would mean getting wet and cold again. His clothes are already damp enough. He throws his feet up on the coffee table. "These feet aren't doing any trotting around in that mess outside!" He lays further back in the loo and turns on the hologram.

A gentleman with a clean face, finely pressed suit, and yellow tie pops up from the projector. "J," he walks around within the box of the hologram's parameters. "We are glad to see you've come to. You will only be here for a little while." He pauses and turns as if to look at him. "Don't try to communicate with me. I won't answer back. I can't really hear you. I know it is you simply because you are the only one in the house and our sensors have you sitting in this room."

J shuffles his body within the loo, scratches his head, and shrugs his shoulders. He looks around the room to check for a camera. As small as they can be, he didn't expect to see anything. "What would I have to say to you?" J changes the transmission to see if the hologram would get something else on the screen. How does this person know him?

With every switch made, the nicely dressed man appears as if the change had never been made and continues from where he left off. The background of each channel is the only thing changing within the dimensions of the hologram. A white room, cactus, unrealistic trees, and so on. Each switch only temporarily displaying what is probably supposed to be there. Eventually, everything fades back into the white room.

"You have been brought here…"

Click.

"Because you were found, at a sight of a major crime, also involving a member of your immediate family which we were unable to save. We have reasons to believe that you may have had something to do with killing your own grandfather."

"I would never kill my own grandfather! Are you crazy?" J is ecstatic. How could anybody accuse him of killing his own grandfather? Click.

"Our resources tell us that you are, in part, responsible for what has happened at 36001 5th Street. We only want to ask why you would kill your own family." A loo, of his own, rises into the hologram and he sits. "Relaxation is key right now, Mr. J." He sits down, grabs a drink from the air next to him, and sips it.

"Relax? I don't even know where I am? How am I supposed to be comfortable enough to just sit back and relax? Maybe I could've before you came along, but now, it is even more difficult." Just moments ago, he had been relaxed enough to escape reality and set himself into the comforts of this home. Accuse me of killing my grandfather, then tell me I should relax. Ludicrous!

"Mr. J. We realize that you are not in a fair position here, but what is fair? Are you fair? Can you truly be the one to define fair? You must be! Besides, you are the one who wiped out thousands of innocent civilian lives, hundreds of our own men, and caused billions in damage repair. Most of which will never be repaired. Is this what you define as fair? How could you have done this knowing that you would be taking so many innocent lives?" He leans forward in his loo, as if trying to look J directly in the eyes. "Fair?"

"What?" The man said he wouldn't be able to communicate with the hologram. How could he know if J were looking at it or sifting through the house to find food? The man said he wouldn't be able to hear J. Now, he seems to be directly responding to him.

"We have chosen to keep you here for a little while because of the reputation you have given yourself. It makes you safer. Have you defined fair yet? Maybe your defining it, is why you are here. Some want you dead! Others think you are going to be able to 'show them the way.' We just want to make sure that Justice meets her mate. You may be wondering what we are going to do with you. Good question."

"Who is this guy? What did I do?" In the back of his mind, he knows what he has done. He is currently boggling through how he was caught. Explosion... Darkness... Red Light... He can't recall anything. Grandfather's death had been planned along with all the rest of this mess. Planned and executed to the key, with a little delay due to incompetent trainees.

"We don't know what you are capable of and we don't care. We have a leash on you, and it won't happen again. Now that you've been caught, we are aware of your potential. What we do want is to figure out how. How could a kid and some fool of an old man do this?" Multiple flashes of the events recreate themselves in the hologram. Individual buildings are seen transforming themselves into heaps of garbage. Explosion after explosion punches through the rubble. This is understandable. This is what was supposed to happen. Oddly, some of them aren't from the area where the bomb went off. Extra events seem to be punishing parts of the city beyond what they had decided. There was a reason for taking out that site. Destroy the central building. They had no reason to shoot beyond the perimeter of their bomb.

"What?!" J jumps up out of his loo. "He's not a fool! You stupid bastard! You didn't even know we were coming! We hit you hard! You don't even know him!" He grabs a vase on a nearby surface and flings it at the hologram and it shatters on the stone wall behind the projection. "How can you expect to solve anything if you don't take the time to figure out who you are dealing with?" He pauses. Frustration is building through his blood. He can see his grandfather standing amongst the people in his basement. When he spoke to them, he would continue to increase in anger and build in rage. Through this, he can see where his

61

own rage comes from. "We aren't responsible for all of this!"

"Excuse me, J." The man is now leaning against a pole in the middle of the projection. The vase has obviously not fazed him. His arms are crossing his body and his torso is facing J. "Our sensors are telling me that your heart rate and breathing have increased exponentially. Your blood pressure is on the rise. You should calm yourself and stop lying."

"Well what the hell do you expect?!" J snatches the transmitter from the arm of the loo and presses the power button. It doesn't shut off.

"What do you expect?!" The man asks with a slight smirk. It doesn't work. The hologram flickers but remains functioning. "We control this, as we do your future. Only those things, in this cell, that we want to work will be useful."

"Excuse me... You need to not do that..." He jams his finger down on the button again.

"What?" He presses the button again. A bolt of electricity shoots out from the transmitter and stings his arm. The transmitter falls to the ground, and J's arm jerks back from the sudden jolt. "Ah!" He grabs his arm and rubs it to sooth some of the stabbing pain. It feels like his body has just made an attempt to bring itself back to life. "What the..."

"Don't worry kid. You shouldn't lose your arm or anything else. It should only be numb for a little while. Oh... Don't try to unplug the system either. It may be life threatening. When you are ready to join me, I can get back to what is going on here. You shouldn't be irrational. Thought we taught you better than that. To be irrational, is to create illogical thought. Creating illogical thought turns you into an enemy of the State. Oh... You're already there. Sorry 'bout that."

J continues to rub the sting out of his arm as he sits himself back into the loo. If they wanted his attention, they got it. He can still feel the energy flowing through his bones. The shock numbing his nerves vibrates through his body.

"You see, kid. You are in a world of trouble. You don't want to challenge us. Everyone knows who you are. They are also capable of knowing where you may be. You're not a secret. It won't matter how long we keep you out of the system. What you've done is too memorable." Another hologram pops up within the original. "The news has covered your story for us perfectly. They've all demonized you. So, we will eventually let you back into society. For now, we have other plans. When you go back, you won't last long. We don't intend to allow it. Although, I don't think you have us to fear. If you adhere to our plans, we may be able to save your pathetic little life."

A smaller hologram begins showing J continuous clips of newscasts from around the world.

"As you can see, the events of yesterday have brought us to this man." A photo of J is shone upon the backdrop of the mini hologram. "He simply goes by the name J. No one knows if he has a last name or even if he has a family in support of the government. After all, his only known family was killed by his own actions. What kind of person stoops to kill his own people? How could anyone, like this man, have anything positive to do for our great developing country? He can't! He is the nemesis of our society! Gladly and heroically, Captain James was able to bring this man in immediately after the event had happened." A picture of the Captain and his XTR3 covers the screen.

"It was nothing." James stands next to the body of J lying on the ground where he had been captured. "I knew he was up to something and I simply did my job to bring him in for committing, what may turn out to be, the crime of the century. I never realized I would be claiming the prize criminal. It was almost too easy." He laughs and the crowd of reporters roar their approval.

On the full sized hologram, the landscape of Michitah, the island overlooking 5th Street, could be seen beyond J and his dupod. J watches himself burning the blueprints in the trash. Grasping the entirety of the atmosphere surrounding the hologram, he could see the innocent people wandering the streets. He could pick out some of the extra squad vehicles pulling up to the house just before it blew. Children were playing in the park across from his grandfather's home, with their parents watching over them.

Living through the event, J remembers how fast everything had been over. He didn't remember seeing any children. He couldn't bring himself to see why any of them would have been there. He knows that it is against the law for anybody to be within a certain area surrounding a raid. He also knows that the government has influence over what is shown on their waves. When the police had a specified number of vehicles in the area, everyone had to stay out of the way. They had to create an imaginary bubble between themselves and any proceedings.

Watching this event happen all over again, he had almost begun to wish he had never done it. Although, he knows he can't take back time. Can't correct the mistakes made. What were they expecting to accomplish by showing him this? If his grandfather were still around, he'd tell J *the lives taken were sacrifices to liberty and freedom from an unforgiving democratic government gone wrong. Do not show regret. Your objectives have been met. Victory will, someday, belong to the people again.* So, hopefully, he is right.

Unfortunately, he is not here. Instead, the events have occurred as they were planned. He was supposed to die, and anyone getting in the way was to go along with it. Those people weren't there when the house blew. Now they would be martyrs to a cause. The tape has obviously been tampered with. It had to be.

"Kid, you think this is bad?" He waits. "It isn't. You should hear what your people are saying about you. Let's touch a few of those channels."

"My people? These aren't my people! It's not like I am leading some sort of Populist movement or a party in opposition to another. My people?"

On the hologram, block after block pops up talking about him and how he had single handedly taken upon himself, a war with the country, and lost.

CBD NEWS

"Is this a strike to our freedom? Have the people finally spoken out against an aggressor far greater than the government? What will they do to him when they find him? They won't let something like this go unanswered. None of us here at CBD want to be in his shoes."

ABE NEWS

"We here at ABE have never seen anything like this. What was this man thinking?" A picture of J pops up. "Take a good look at him. I have a gut feeling you will be able to deal with him on your own. This type of crime will not be single handedly dealt with by the government. They will let him go so that we can let him feel our wrath. Thank Big Brother for capital punishment, and pray that the poor soul dies before we get him."

She is right. The people are now able to do whatever they want to when a person kills. What will be done with J? Will he be fed to them as many others have been?

WASHINGTON DIRECT

"We are incredibly proud of the great Captain James and what he has done to protect us from an evil such as this.

It is rather unfortunate that he couldn't have been caught before hand."

Other stations are showing mobs of people holding hate posters.

'Execute him!'

'Let him boil!'

'Feed him to the people!'

"As you can see kid, you aren't favored. The public hates you! That's why you won't be here long. We're going to watch them all kill you. It'll be fun. We'll even record it to set future examples." He pauses to let these horrid statements settle onto J's ears. Then he continues, "but if you help us, it won't have to end that way." He leaves the hologram and the deck blacks out. "Transmission ending."

VII

"It's not my fault those kids died! No one was supposed to be out there! We had it planned! They all knew they weren't supposed to be there! We had it planned! Did they not get the messages?!"

Grandfather would have said the same. "We had it planned! What's done is done! Their choices will become their consequences! We will not be held accountable! Then, if they die, they don't support the cause. If not, traitors deserve to die. Or they died, simply so that the cause will be able to fight on. They lied to us and ratted us out. What happened to their loyalty? These people were supposed to be backing us and the cause! At least up until it all went through. If they don't support the cause, they must have forgotten it!"

Is it up to me to revive it? Am I the only one left? How could they have abandoned what they believe in?" Through his mind, J is working over the unbelievable stories he has just witnessed. So many... Masses of people supported what was supposed to be a justified ideal. If they don't support what they believed in, then there is no cause.

J gets up from the loo and walks directly to the only other visible door, which he believes, should lead him outside. Go through the door, he came in from, and he just ends up in the dark cold room again, with nowhere to go. This time he wants to leave. Leave, escape to the 'dead zones', and he should be safe. He could live off the land. Even though it is contaminated, he could still find a way to survive. There has to be a way to get out of here. It's locked. This time it isn't as simple as just unlocking it and waltzing to freedom. It has either been locked from the outside or there isn't even an actual door and the knob is just a fragment of his imagination placed there to mock his intelligence and laugh in his face as he desperately turns it in anticipation of escape.

"I have to get out of here. How can I actually trust that all of this is real? There can't be any truth to what I have seen. It all ran so smoothly. They have manipulated the system! That's the only way they could possibly show me that. Those people weren't there when it happened!" He continues talking aloud, in his own defense. Maybe they will still be listening as they are monitoring him.

Was this the loss of a family member or a plan gone wrong? What else will he be experiencing? If only he could get out of this place... Or, when they "let him go"... What will happen? There has to be more. No matter what the little hologram man says. Not many "rebels" make it out of a place like this.

Jimmy Newcombe was granted freedom and murdered by a mob shortly after. His crime was no where near as severe as J's. He had hacked into a few computers putting some big businesses out of operation in 2045. Grandfather had the theory that his murder had been staged. Or, they were paid to get rid of him.

Hertford was lynched, by his own family, in the arena. A newer form of execution, modeled after a civilization of some 2,000 years ago. Hertford voiced his opinion against the system. He didn't agree with giving his relative's home to the government after the resident had died.

Others, like Jones and Maddey were killed in their sleep before they could get their release handed to them the next day. They robbed a bank. Still, nothing in comparison to what he had done. None of the executions match the crimes committed.

Is the same set up for J? Would the house implode and spread his remains just as he had killed so many himself? Would the mob take him to the arena and beat him with sticks? One thing for sure, he isn't going to wait around to find out what they are going to do. Allowing himself to remain pinned where he cannot defend himself against the odds of what they can create. That would be suicide.

There is only one way out. He has to get through the roof and into the wet darkness beyond. The holes in the roof are, in some places, large enough to allow for his escape. As long as there isn't anyone out there and they have underestimated his reaction to their plans, he should be okay to slip through the hole and down the shingles without being noticed. How would he be able to reach it?

J decides to push the hologram projector into the dark room so that he might be able to get high enough. Then he can jump and grab the ceiling and lift himself through one of these holes. He looks around to find a spot where he can do exactly this. The ceiling is lower than he thought it would be.

He drags the hologram projector to the middle of the dark wet prison room where there is a spot large enough for two of him to fit through. He jumps up on top of the projector. He squats down and pushes himself into the air as high as his legs will allow him to go. J grabs the edge of the roof and hangs on. It's sharp, slippery, and wet. He struggles to pull himself up and look outside. Remarkably, he doesn't cut himself. The edge of the broken ceramic tiles are jagged and chipped in all the wrong places. Rain pelts him from above. He sees nothing. Darkness surrounds the prison and shines forth midnight, giving away no immediate exit.

"This is too easy."

J pulls himself, waist level, to the roof, then all of the way out. He rolls out onto the cold porcelain shingles. They crackle under his pressure; the weight from his body is bearing down on them. He can feel himself slightly slipping on the wet shingles. He brings himself to an upright stance and looks around again. Straining his eyes to see something through the darkness, he sees nothing. His vision isn't good enough to see through the blankets of rain. The only thing J can see is the side of the mountain that he is basically standing on. The room, he has emerged from, is completely surrounded by rock. Even if he had been able to go through that door, he may have been thrown into a maze of caves and tunnels for which he had no flashlight or way of navigating.

Beyond the roof, there is no sign of life. At least there is nothing he can hear or see beyond the noise of the storming rain. No thunder exists. Nor has it been present at any other part of the night. All sound seems to be rebounding from the punishment of the cold rain. A glow is present from a light at the edge of the roof. The shingles appear to be the only protection offered for it. Even with this light glimmering, there isn't much of a reflection from anything besides its dim radiance, covered by the thickness of fog.

He looks and feels around for a good spot to jump off the roof. He isn't sure how far down the ground is. The dark and rainy night isn't exactly allowing him to see anything. This would be so much easier, if the rain would stop. Conveniently, he decides to use the side of the mountain wrapped over the back half of the house. Placing his feet in small holes descending the slant of the mountain, he works his way down to the ground.

"I need to get out of here. They've got to be coming some time soon. If they're not already laughing at me through their lenses, they soon will be. They have to know I'm out here. How could you just leave a criminal to escape so easily? Where are the dogs?" Talking to himself isn't making his escape faster. If he is being chased by dogs, he realizes that he now needs to put a lot of space between himself and the prison.

J heads down the slope of the mountain. Continuously worrying about whether or not there is a drop off, finding safe harbor is his goal. Because he doesn't know where he is, uncertainty of safety weighs heavily on his mind. "Take one thing at a time," he reassures himself. He has to make it off this hill and through the night, first. If the night and steady downpour can't be beaten, he won't have to worry about his captors.

Knowing that the watchful eyes of his predators are possibly all around him, he is cautious to protect himself. If they come from the darkness, where will he run? If the stone opens up, swallows him, and everyone on the inside laughs at and beats him to death, he would be done. No honest chance to flee. No apparent opportunity to run. He would be finished.

Finally, he reaches ground. He feels his feet touch solid hard soil. His shoes are wet and his toes numb. The rain, still beating on J's back, has become like hundreds of cold merciless daggers. J begins to shiver as he wanders through the dark. Concern of anyone jumping out of the night slowly fades away. The coldness not only numbs his body, but his senses as well. He seems unaware of his surroundings. The shivering has him out of sync with the rest of his body. He manages to find trees. He uses these as leverage aiding him down the unforgiving slope of the steep path he is unable to avoid. Occasionally, he stumbles over a fallen tree. He is blind, guided only by the slope of the hill and silhouettes of stumps that he can't miss tripping over. When he falls on his face, he slides a foot before he can grasp another tree and pull himself to his feet, only to fall again.

Traveling down the slope isn't allowing him to leave the rain any faster. Yet, he continues to push forward, knowing that something else is out there that is worse than what he is facing right now. Feeling around for what he can find to break his fall, he searches desperately for an alternative route off this hill. Maybe he would find a road or path, which has been traveled often. Hopefully he wouldn't have to walk for too much longer.

"This is insane! I'm hungry, wet, and an army of people are out there somewhere waiting for me to pop my head around the corner. I'm not going to be their bait!"

Lack of leaves on the trees due to the late Fall season, makes it so that shelter from the rain is impossible. He dodges, from tree to tree, pausing under the slanted ones only as often as he needs. Maybe there he would be able to dry off some of the water engulfing his body and soaking his skin. Water still finds a way to drip along the contours of his spines and sends chills across all of his nerve endings. Staying in any one spot, for too long, is unwise.

In the distance, through the darkness, J can see a glimmering light. This becomes a sudden shot of hope that he might be able to escape this cursed world of ice like rain. A light often means there might be someone out there. This could be either good or bad. What if this person is one of them? Go to the light and be free of those who may or may not be pacing themselves through the woods after him. The light could be the bait luring J to his captors waiting in their foxholes to destroy him. Or, on the other hand, there could be a fire and warmth waiting for him inside some privileged beings' home. Hopefully, they wouldn't be a part of the system. Maybe they would let him come in. Maybe they would feed him.

A chance has to be taken. With some luck, he may be looking down at the gnarling mouth of a rabid dog with the owner on the other end of the chain. If he is in no man's land, that wouldn't be impossible. Anything could happen out here. If not, his journey to freedom would be forced to a screeching halt as the butt of a gun slams against his head and knocks him unconscious.

Despite the chance that his flight could abruptly end, J decides to take the chance. He aims his sights for the light.

He is determined to set it right. He has to get out of the cold. Stunned to see how he had come about this mess, he finds himself struggling with what he had been taught in school and the words of his grandfather. "Support the Government, follow the rules, and listen to your elders." They always kept you on the up spin. They never allowed you to know the reality of what you may have to face after school. They never let you in on how to handle life after graduation. They always claimed to be preparing you for it. They just want to make sure you're not going to do anything that opposes the way the government runs. They brainwash you. Yet, they never tell you what will happen if you run out on the system. You find out by either doing it or seeing the examples that they show you through the holograms and screens plastered on billboards painted across the cities.

People will always put down the government. You can only learn about the reality of its power through those who have experienced what it has done to them. Or, you find out when the exterminators arrive. Yet, another group J would have never known about unless his grandfather had let him in on the secret. He never believed in them. He thought them urban legends. J had never expected them to actually swarm his grandfather's home. He had been warned and prepared the bomb for the day that they may have come, but he never really expected them to do it. J expected that his grandfather would die before they came. So many times, he wanted the exterminators to be a conspiracy set up by pranksters with a dark sense of humor.

After all, they weren't real. None of his teachers ever mentioned anything about them. None of the students ever talked about neighbors being invaded by them. Yet, it all happened to him. He is here now, soaking in frigid water and looking for a way to get out of it. Wondering if there is actually a way to evade the future and knowing that there isn't.

So, what do you do? Who do you trust? Follow their rules? What makes the next person any better? Overthrow the President and his people? You'd have to take over the entire system, from the ground up. This has been done before. Another will come to control. Will they be any better? Will they fight for the people or be another in a line of control freaks punishing you with more rules and restrictions that will take a lifetime to force onto those people who are resisting.

Crossing a small creek, he could see the change in rainfall from the splashing in the stream. Even though the rain is beginning to lighten up, he can't feel the difference. His body aches from the cold. His sodden clothes straining against his movement. It is night, and the darkness definitely welcomes a colder atmosphere. Maybe he would find warmth in the light. Hopefully, he isn't walking in circles. Hopefully, the cold hasn't drawn him back to the place he is trying to run from. He can't see beyond the shack. Engulfed by the wind and rain, he presses forward to answer his questions. He needs to be sure of an escape. He wants to be confident that he is still sane. He needs to get to that light.

The ground is softer on this side of the creek. Maybe grass wasn't present here and mud was giving way beneath his feet. Or, the rain had softened the sod so that he would float on each step. Either way, it didn't matter to him. He feels that this side of the stream is more promising. This side of the creek is not as slanted. It seems as if the creek is where all of the rain, from the hill, flows. As he crosses the ground, he can see that someone had set up some sort of an irrigation system where the creek empties into a field of trenches next to rows of mud hills. There is an extensive assortment of plowed fields sprawling out in front of him as far as the light would allow him to see. As the rain ceases, J can see more of what he is approaching.

A small light shines over the corner of a small cabin just a few yards from a pool of water, on the edge of a walkway. From a distance, J can see that the cabin has been styled after one of the log cabins from a time in the past when lumber was a popular means of building homes. Its authenticity could be doubted though. There aren't many of these around any more, and it is illegal to cut down trees for any use. Yet, there are trees everywhere the eye can see. Typically, anyone who owns one of these homes had one of two things.... money or power. In J's case, he hopes the person has neither.

Fumbling over his future actions, J isn't sure what to do next. When he gets to the cabin, should he be polite and knock on the door? Should he try to find a dry place to relax, away from the home? Or, should he skip the place entirely and try to find somewhere else to hide for the night? Besides, an ignited light could mean a lot of trouble. Every choice has a consequence and one always out weighs the other. Not every consequence is desired.

If the home is owned by anyone who has anything to do with the dungeon he has left, then he knows he can be in over his head. Yet, what can he possibly walk into that would bring him more trouble than what he has already faced?

Sifting through the field and walking in the trenches so that he doesn't damage any food or leave any easily noticeable tracks, he finally makes it to the shack. Evidence of another soul present in the area does not exist. There aren't any footprints or trails made from people traveling a path too often. Except for the loose stones from where someone had sped off in the other direction, and the light shining on the outside of this cabin, there isn't much of anything left that tells J that someone had been here.

"Anybody here?" J builds up enough courage to call out for someone and break the sinister silence. No answer. In fact, the rain has stopped falling, and the silence is now more chilling than the cold itself. He tries again, almost yelling. He is sure to get something.

Cold wind blows, making the outer door slap itself against the frame. Its screen is ripped and torn from years of the same monotonous banging. It appears as if no one has tended to it for years. The frame, where the screen door continuously thumps, is chipped and worn. The paint is old, faded, and cracked. Holes are present in the side of the home where the mudding has been damaged from the weathering. One could stand on the inside, turn a light on, and people on the outside could watch their shadow moving around within. J can imagine the wind pouring through the cracks and chilling the back of a person's spine as if a ghostly presence were amongst him.

This isn't your average ordinary shack. Homes in the city are never allowed to look like this. The city either cleans your home for a small fee, or the owners keep them up on their own. "A clean home is the symbol of a truly structured community." At least that's what Madaggan always wanted people to believe. Grandfather always considered this as one of the ways that government is allowed to keep an eye on you. Either you are outside, among the cameras, or they are working in your yard and watching your home. It is also another way for government to continuously milk you for your money and fund their own causes, which, according to Grandpa, no one knows about. Oddly, this place has been overlooked for a long time.

J walks in through the swinging screen door. A bear skin rug lies in the middle of the floor with its eyes glowing from the reflection of the moonlight seeping in either from a window or the cracks in the walls. It startles him at first glance. Silhouettes of odd shapes and unfamiliar possessions shine their dreary shadows onto the walls. More reflections, of eyes, are staring down upon him. Clustered with darkness, he notices some objects hanging on the walls and brings himself closer so that he can see them better.

On one wall, J sees a traditional family. Black and white photos, of people staring blankly at the camera, are hung organized in a symmetrical pattern. None of them are smiling. All of them looking like they are either unhappy or too serious to be able to smile. Cars easily recognized as being over two hundred years old, sit in their picture frames as real as life. J can't tell specifically what class they belong to. That part, of history, never really interested him when he was in school. Those pieces would never matter because they could never be repeated.

He can see that the pictures seem to be organized so that they pass through the lives of those people within the photographs themselves. Young children are seen growing up before his eyes. Families grow together and apart as each member moves away and starts their own lives. The expanse of people could have been placed onto an incredibly in depth family tree. J could only guess that the family tree was that of Madaggan's. There were no names other than this. None of the photos shared the secret of who each individual person was or where they went off too. The only word, Madaggan, was placed in the center of the wall.

J knows the name, better than he knows the cars, because he hears it so often. Madaggan is supposed to be the man his grandfather blamed for the present state of the world. It is also the same person that the schools thought of as a martyr to society. "Differences of opinion influencing the way we think. Thinking in ways that can get a person killed." Common words often quoted whenever he is mentioned.

The other three walls are in color and hologram. Color pictures are better, of course. The little bit of light, coming through the cracks and windows, is slightly enough for him to observe the memories of this family as he strolls around staring into the eyes of people he has never known. Finally, J sees a name of two men in one of the color photos. Richards and Madaggan standing side-by-side staring back at whomever the photographer had been. Madaggan is the taller, better built man. He is young and tireless. Most of the pictures, near the end of the wall, show him rising through the ranks in the military. As he ages, J can see how his life might have been harder. Maybe Madaggan met up with an event, which he had never expected to confront. Maybe the difficulties of leading a nation into war affected his health in such a way that he could only wear down.

Even these pictures are old. This man had been caught posing with many of the historical figures, which J can recall from his schoolbooks. He sees a few famous and well-decorated Generals, President McCullough, and a number of foreign faces.

Yet, who is this Madaggan guy? Grandfather had always told him that Madaggan was the man who made everything evil. "He is the direct descendent of the serpent." His teachers were always praising the man like he single-handedly founded the country. "He fought for this country and changed it so that we have what we enjoy today. He prevented a war from destroying our country." In a sense, this is also exactly what grandfather was saying. On the other hand, grandfather was spinning how the man had destroyed the country. So, who is he? Who do you believe?

J stands back from the wall and looks, in awe, at how many of these photographs are finally coming in focus for him. There are more than he had thought. The moon must be hitting just the right angle because the light is almost perfectly lighting up the faces of the pictures. He is finally able to get the whole perspective of the pictures without having to stand so close or worry about shadowing out the parts he might like to see. There are more to them than he is taking in. The color of the pictures is set up to display the former flag of the United States. He can see the stars in the white of the uniforms many of the people had been wearing. The frames of many of the pictures set up the stripes of it. Boldly... Entirely... with the flag.

Above him, the flag had been painted into the ceiling. Dry, old, paint, is peeling from years of exposure. Chips, of

78

color lie on the floor where J has been stepping. An extremely dedicated shrine of a family's patriotic feelings, pasted over his head.

What is this that J has stumbled into? J could only imagine that he has broken into some sort of unveiling for that question by standing in the middle of the man's home with Madaggan's name sprawled across the wall to the past. He can't still be alive. Madaggan is a fragment of time in the past. Even if he is alive and noting that he would be the oldest man living, he wouldn't still be living here. In society, he is famous. The people love him. Why would he have given up the continuous rule as President? No one would expect him to have ever even lived in a home like this. This home isn't the typical type for people as well known as him.

The calm of the night is beginning to wear on J. Even though the rain had broken off a while ago, the dripping of water is mesmerizing. J is tired. Scanning the rest of the cabin, he spots a couch, which should have been a piece of illegal furniture. He pulls the dusty sheet off of it. It looks comfortable and inviting. J sits on it. He sinks in the cushions. It's even more comfortable than it looks. Beating the dust off the sheet, he covers himself and lies himself down to sleep. It is unbelievably easy for J to doze off. Comfort overrides consciousness, and sleep becomes the engulfing power to which he submits himself.

VIII

"Sir! He has gone. Would you like us to continue to follow as we had planned?"

"As planned, Junior. You know what we have to do. Don't let him out of your sight."

Junior turns himself from the Captain to the control panel, spins a few knobs, flips a group of switches, and a monitor kicks on. J appears on the screen as he is walking on the roof of the building he has just escaped from. It isn't a well-defined picture of him. The rain and darkness make it so that the image of J is fuzzy and delayed. The delay is caused from the inability to have access to all of the satellites they would like to be able to use.

Unfortunately, those satellites were taken out of the sky during Madaggan's War. Yet, the camera's infrared sensors are capable of slightly reducing the blur and shaping out the form of his body from its own heat. What little heat can be generated and sensed from such a distance in the cold weather. He is slowly moving across the screen, fumbling with his steps like a young child.

"Keep that monitor on, Junior. I want to track him until he crosses the river. We need to make sure that is where he goes. And don't forget to contact Matt. He is our only chance right now. He knows this kid."

"No problem, Sir."

Junior taps a few more buttons, turns a couple more dials, and another small screen pops up in the lower left hand corner.

"Hello?" A voice comes from this monitor.

"Matt, are you ready?"

"To serve and deliver. I'll even wrap the gift and put a bow on it."

"Good. He is on the move. You know what to do."

"Why couldn't I have just picked him up at the cave? It would've saved us all a lot of time."

"No questions. We have our reasons. You, do your job! Leave the planning to us. If you don't get this done, you will be dealt with." Being 'dealt with' is as simple as being demoted. Usually it meant time in prison among those who were put there by him. Outside of prison, he can deal with them one at a time. Inside, he might not make it back.

The image of Matt disappears and Junior begins flipping through the several different cameras at his command. As J journeys through the night, he is expected to go in and out of focus for each camera. Junior needs to make sure that J is on the right path and that nobody else is going to interfere with the operation. Stumbling from tree to tree, his movement is sloppy. Junior begins wondering if something is wrong with J. Not that he would be concerned to any emotional extent. They only care that he makes it to the pick up point alive. If J doesn't make it to their expected destination, it throws everything else off. Then, they have to re-plan their mode of infiltration and recovery.

He seems to be roaming around pointlessly. Almost as if he has lost all care of the fact that the government is after him. Any average citizen knows that they should fear them. They all know that they come from everywhere. What he doesn't know, is what they have planned for him, and how much he is going to be used by them.

"He's not doing much, sir. He has no sense of direction. I think he doesn't know where he is."

"Send another message to Matt and let him know the delivery is going to be a little delayed. We don't want him getting bored while waiting for him to get there."

"Yes, sir." Instead of bringing the second screen up, he places a pair of headphones onto his ears. These sets consist of two plugs for the ears and a clear mouthpiece that fastens to the skin through the use of miniature suction cups. Being verbally operated, the set responds almost immediately to his voice, "555-1754-82." A dial tone sounds. Digits start plugging back into his ears and it starts buzzing.

"Yeah?" Matt's voice breaks the buzz. "Whatcha need?"

"The delivery is going to be delayed."

"I see. I'll wait. This place is kind of interesting. I can just sit back and relax while I'm waiting."

"Keep your eyes open. You know that we can't see you anymore. We can't afford any screw ups."

Matt wanders around the cabin where he is waiting for his contact. Before he was called, he had been enjoying a sensuous moment in the spa. His muscles had been receiving a pounding from the jets. A moment of true relief from the day he had just gone through.

He barely made it home from his last job and here they are already calling him up to do another. He expected the little guy to break a lot easier. The hacker shouldn't have known that he was on his way. Instead, the twerp had been waiting. When Matt walked through the front door, he didn't see the wooden stick coming at him. That maggot got the best of him. Bruises outline the narrow curve of the stick where it had broken across the bridge of his nose. Luck was on his side when his nose didn't break. The surprise had only set him back momentarily. Yet, the man didn't act soon enough, and his prey didn't get away. They never get away.

The pleasure he had been receiving from that pool of warm pressure blown water felt soothingly good to his aching muscles. Melting away in that swirl would have easily been comparable to being engulfed in his bedding. He is tired and the thought of being at home, in bed, is making him want to fall asleep. It should be okay to rest for a while.

He finds his way to the antique couch in the middle of the room. As he punches the sheet cover, a film of dust rises into the air. He pinches a corner of the sheet and pulls hard, revealing a soft and comfortable looking place for him to lay his aching body. He sits himself down and takes in the welcoming feeling as it molds to fit his exhausted body. Within minutes, he is out. He becomes lost in his own mind, his soul overcome by peace, and existence breaks from reality.

The silence of the evening allows the darkness to welcome his exhaustion. Sleep could not have been more rewarding for anyone who had worked as hard as he did today. It isn't often that Matt gets to enjoy a good rest. Rarely ever would someone, in his career, even make an attempt to sleep without the protection of a secure facility. Matt, in particular, lives with the continuous threat of being hunted down by one of the families of a person he has knocked off. It's a risk taken. Out here, he has no one to fear. He's gone through this procedure a couple dozen times. Never has he come across another person, besides the person he is looking for.

Close encounters are extremely rare, but not unheard of. In one such case, Matt had to wipe out a hacker who broke into the computer programs and left explosive bugs. It didn't take long for Matt to track the guy down. When he arrived at this man's home, he had also been waiting. Another unpredictable incident, that could have been worse than today's event.

This man chose a different way to beat the system. He rigged his entire home with heavy explosives. He was ready for the entire force to come after him. He was so good at what he did, Big Brother believed that the man had hacked into the camera network and watched the plans for his extermination taking place. Without a chance to fight, the man had yanked a detonation device from his shirt pocket. Caressing it for the strength it possessed, the man plainly grinned as Matt pulled up to the house. Matt had just seen the man's wife coming through the front door, onto the porch. He knew what he was going to have to do to the man and almost began to feel a trace of pity for the lady.

When he saw the trigger, he barely had enough time to protect himself from the implosion of his vehicle's framework. He couldn't believe a man would be so desperate as to kill his family to protect himself. He remembered how beautiful the lady looked. Her summer dress had easily draped the features of her body. A wide unknowing smile spread from ear to ear.

Unfortunately, because Matt was protecting himself, he was even less capable of saving this poor lady's life. Saving her was never truly an option. Even if he had wanted to, he would have had to figure out a way to save her from the detonator. Looking on the bright side, he didn't have to lay a hand on the man. He did himself in and the press issued it as a suicide. They caught the whole thing on their network. An easy day's work spent sitting on his pockets. No paperwork had to be filed.

IX

"I can't believe what I am seeing! Do you see this?" Scott had been stroking his keyboard and playing with a holographic mouse so that he could bring his newest discovery to life. It isn't often that something like this happens out here. "We have the kid!"

"Which kid is that?"

"You know... the kid!"

"Okay, I know the kid down the street. The news kid is always great to stop and talk to. There was once this other kid that I kicked really hard and he..."

"No, you idiot! A couple months ago, the police, somewhere on the East coast, had brought in a kid that destroyed an entire city block along with the Central Building for the Fed. This catastrophe shut down the Fed's Atlantic operations long enough for some of our people along the Appalachian range to figure out some of their positions. They also say he's the one that wiped out the President."

"No way! Let me see! This can't be the kid from Citru." Angel isn't much of a push over. She never believes anything unless she has either experienced it or seen it with her own eyes. A discovery like this would make their efforts so much easier. If they could get this kid to back their cause, they would be home free and the country would soon be united again. Life isn't much for living in the dead zones. Zone 6 is even less of an inhabitable zone than most of the others.

Madaggan's War created a lot of dead zones in the former United States. The zones are areas thought to be contaminated with toxic radiation. Because of Madaggan's War, the entire country had been split into blotches and patches of inhabitable and uninhabitable lands. Even though years have gone by, since the war, and the government knows there are survivors, not all of the zones had been tested for toxins. Everything was based on the assumption of hazardous living areas.

So, either to save time or prevent chaos from within the cities, they hunt down the survivors. If they are found, they are killed. If people leave the city and stumble into a zone, they too are eliminated. Secrecy is the key to their survival. Don't let anyone know where you've been or where you are from.

"What was his name again?"

"Been a couple of months, I thought he would have been executed already. They usually never live long."

"Good thing Toad was able to send those codes through before they got to him. He's a master unknown."

With the codes, that Toad had sent through the underground, any set up system could hack into the government's mainframe, take advantage of their cameras, and receive transmissions from their limited radio network. The absence of satellites makes it easier for them to get into whatever information they may ever need. It's all done through the old cable that had connected the world over a 100 years ago.

Just before Toad had taken his own life, he wanted to give the people that government thought about the least, the upper hand. Living in the zones created restrictions in society. Restrictions limiting so many from ever seeing their families. The system isn't willing to accept the fact that the war was survivable by those who were not protected. Toad created a code that would allow those, who lived in the zones, to converse with the rest of the world. It sent out programs, which no one has been able to detect or prevent from spreading. With this, many of the zones were able to see what the rest of the functioning world sees.

"Is that really him?"

"I can't tell, he looks a little sluggish."

"Our sensors, in the old Madaggan house, are picking up some movement. We'd better get there."

"There hasn't been anyone around here since 3 years ago." Scott examines the map of Zone 6. "After what we did to that guy, I can't believe they are sending more of them."

"Madaggan was a pretty wicked man." Angel pulls herself from the screen, where J is putting a lot of effort into staying on his feet, and she studies the map of Madaggan's property with Scott. "What do you suppose we should do?"

"What choice do we have?" Scott zooms out from the dot bleeping inside the house and points to another dot moving slowly toward the house. "The kid's only chance is to make it across that stream and to this house. He won't be there for a while and anyone in that house will ruin our chances of getting him on our side. Whoever is there," he points at the first dot, "isn't one of ours. Anybody in that old house can't have anything good to do with Zone 6. What do you think we should do?"

They can't be seen. If they cross the stream, and convince J to follow them, they could give themselves away. In order to avoid crossing the stream, they have to make the cabin safe for their new comer. If they are seen, troops will be sent. With that unwanted arrival, comes the end of life as they know it.

Angel pulls a wire from her sleeve and wraps it from her ear to her mouth. "Damn, no one's answering! I was hoping someone else could go to check this out. Can't believe this! No one is ever around the station when we need them there."

"They've probably just stepped away for a bit. Can't expect them to sit in the cubicle all day." The cubicle is a tree house on the western edge of the Zone.

"Looks like we're making a visit to the old Madaggan home." Angel places the wire back into her sleeve, ignoring Scott's pity, and pulls him from the screen. "We have to move fast. If he thinks anyone is there, he'll probably run."

"What's the plan?" She always has a plan. She always seems to dictate the run of events as they unfold. It's not like they have a lot of conflicts in 6, but when they do arise, she always seems to be at the head of it. Scott simply submits to it. There doesn't seem to be any reason to try and be the controlling one. Being in charge, could mean a person's life. Why would he want that responsibility? When she says move, he just fits into place and runs with the events at hand.

"We have to protect our future by saving that kid! If he is who you say he is, we have to get him here. If he isn't, we can use him to our advantage."

Literally running like the wind, Angel and Scott grab their Air Boards and fly as fast as they can to get to the Madaggan house. Air Boards are the way to get around in the zones; especially in the forests. Because they are so small, a person can easily maneuver through the trees and escape any immediate threat. The cities used to use them as a main source of transportation. Gas had failed to be abundant enough to support the continued use of the antique gas engine. For a period of time, before Madaggan's War, the use of magnets placed throughout the city, became a way of moving Air Boards and vehicles of the sort. Eventually the board's technology developed so that it could be operated without magnetic dependence.

Gas had been conserved and mined in Alaska for one reason only. "Push America ahead of the world as the only

Super Power." Madaggan planned to wait and watch the rest of the world suffocated their fuel resources and continued to ignorantly ship the fuel to the states. He believed they would never know about the abundant supply he had stored for his invasions. He wanted to attack them when they could not fight back. "Conserve our fuel for the good of our future. Because they plot against us, we will be the ones to take it to them! We have to be the first to act! There will be no time to react!"

This is no man's land a.k.a. Zone 6. Madaggan's childhood had been spent in this remote area of the country. It was once a small community of people working hard to make it in life. Now, there isn't much left. He abandoned his home. Zone 6 is deserted because of the war. His war. There is nothing left that allows communication to the outside world because it had been taken down during the war.

Satellite communication was one of the first battles fought as the war started in space. Each satellite, sent into space, had been equipped with lasers and targeting systems to knock others out of the sky when the war began. As this began, poorer countries could only sit and pray that they wouldn't be touched by their neighbor's arsenal.

Only the forgotten and accessible cable line, connect the dead zones to the rest of the outside world. Within Angel and Scott's base, there are Scrubs who live off hacking into the system trying to reassemble the patches of no man's land. Because of Toad's work, this has become much easier. Yet, caution still has to be taken. Anyone entering the dead zones, unannounced, may be eliminated, looked into, or removed from the area, by force.

"Monitor says whoever it is might be sleeping. They have absolutely no idea that we are coming. Jammers must still be stable." Scott tucks his board behind some shrubs and hides the small hand-size monitor in his vest. "Jez ready?"

Angel flips a compact round dish out of her left pocket and holds it out in front of her. "Let's do this!"

Scott pushes the door open and Angel runs in with the Jez out in front of her. Scott comes in from behind and walks over to where the person is found sound asleep. Angel presses the green button on the Jez. A force field forms around the body and begins to shrink. The man lying on the couch wakes up. He tries stretching out. The invisible walls prevent him from doing so and they shock him. He begins thrashing at the walls. Each shock forces him to temporarily pull his arms and legs back into his body. With each recoil of his limbs, the invisible shell shrinks further. A sudden panic overcomes his rest.

"What the... What are you doing?!" His fists continue to flail out in an attempt to break the energy engulfing his body. Each desperate attempt to free himself, is worse than the last. He stares at Scott. His pupils are enlarging either from fear or rage. In this case, both may be the same. This one is too close. How could anyone have snuck up on him without his knowing? Did his assailant know he was coming? Impossible!

Angel and Scott look on and watch as this monster of a man struggles with the Jez's power constantly engulfing him. Its energy closing in on and pushing back his resistance. Like a trapped animal, they could see him continuously changing emotional states. His body is lunging at whatever is touching and choking his limbs. His thrashing is slowly becoming nothing, but every motion has an alternate force programmed to stop the first.

"If he gets loose, this guy could do some damage, Angel."

"Good thing the Jez never lets anyone go. The more a person fights, the higher the voltage of shock sent through his body."

As they can see, he is weakening. His current baby chimp-like curl no longer possesses a threat to either of them. On the other hand, they know he can't be let go. The Jez simply cannot be shut off without restraining him.

Angel reaches into her knee pocket and pulls out a syringe. "He could have killed us both. That is, of course, had he known we were coming. No wonder Toad killed himself. If these are the thugs they send out to do their dirty work, I wouldn't ever want to face one of them."

"Yeah, good thing the little machine held up this time. I always seem to forget how important that toy is." Scott picks up the Jez and deactivates it. "There ya go."

Angel injects the syringe into the neck of this big fellow. "There ya are pussy cat." She squeezes the trigger of the syringe and the blue sleeping juice disappears into his artery. "That should do ya, Tiger. Sweet dreams."

Scott pulls his backpack off and extracts, from it, a small box. "Now to get him out of here before the kid comes." He sets the box down onto the floor of the home. Tapping it on the side, it unfolds several times and turns into a floating flatbed. It easily hovers above the floor in front of the man.

They both take an end of him and lift his heavy carcass onto the stretcher. It isn't an easy task, even though he can't protest his own movement. He easily weighs as much as both of them combined.

"Despite his effort, this one was too easy, Scott."

"Yeah, usually they send the ones that know a little better than to sleep on the job." Scott thumps the man in the head. "We were lucky this time."

"They'll love it when we send this one back." Angel began imagining some of the previous run-ins with the agents. Violence isn't something that the two of them believe in. Usually they box the person up like an animal and hitch the box to the capital. This meant that they got to see the outskirts of the big cities. They would set the box in front of the post office and leave the area quickly. Staying around means that a fellow converted Scab might recognize them. If they are turned in, they will face death or mind control. Neither is better than the other. Either they die, or they become a fixture of the government's forces controlled through mind control and drugs.

Mind control is an option used to find out what they can't see with their tools. A chip is inserted, into the mind, which is undetectable by most current technology. Once they are done with the subject, the chip explodes and they drop to the ground never knowing what they did. So, this is also a death sentence.

"Don't forget, we have to come back for the kid."

"Yeah, no problem. It shouldn't take us long to wrap him up and have someone else send him on his way."

"I hope we don't have to do this to the kid."

X

J awakens from his much needed sleep. The sunlight streaming into the cabin announces the new day. This is the first time he has ever slept on a real couch let alone seen one and it leaves him with an ache in his back. No wonder this furniture is not allowed anymore with complaints like this. Adjusting to this type of bed, might take a while. J however is not prepared to spend much time here. If he stays here too long, they are destined to find him and sleeping on this couch another night wouldn't do his liberty any good or his sore back.

Most homes would have a Loo or an enclosed material filled with beans, feathers, or water. Sometimes a person might be lucky enough to own some of the artificial cotton that forms to the contour of a person's body. This, like wood, is hard to come by because farm land is rare. The loo is definitely more comfortable to sleep on than the couch. Or, at least, artificial cotton is what he is used to sleeping on. The real stuff is a rich man's commodity.

J stretches out his mid section. Then, he throws his feet into the air and touches them with his hands. It feels good to move freely and not have to worry about the troubles haunting his mind. He is surprised that none of it has prevented him from being able to get any sleep last night. They hadn't even come for him when he was most vulnerable.

Throwing his legs off the edge of the couch, he stands up. It must be late morning. The sun is already up and shining brightly in through the windows. Shadows are also cast from the cracks in the walls, where more mud is needed. "Hmm... Must have over slept."

He twists his torso to the left. A boy stands there. Can't be much older than J himself. He whips his head to the right to see that a girl stands there. She is the same height and wears the same clothes as the boy. His body begins aching all over again. Several thoughts flood his brain, but within seconds are pushed out by panic. How long have they been here? When did they come in? Were they watching him sleep? Have they come to take him in? How could he have possibly imagined that they would not have come after him? They just didn't want it to be too much of a surprise. Wait until the prey knows that the predator is ready to strike, then engulf with pain.

"Hey, kid." The boy speaks to him. At least it sounded like it came from him.

Stunned, J looks again to both sides and realizes that the daydream is a reality. He isn't alone. Two people are standing in the room, watching him. He bends at his waist and grabs his ankles. Maybe they won't stay there for long. Maybe they'll just disappear. That would be nice. Just like when you wake up from a dream. Maybe he is just dreaming.

Did they follow him here? Whoever they are, J isn't going to go out without some sort of a fight. He comes back up from his ankles with an even faster twist of his waist than before. He slams his fist into the lower throat region of the unsuspecting boy. Take him down first. He's bigger and might be able to throw a better punch.

"You're not taking me without a fight!"

The boy grasps his throat and coughs his way slowly to the ground. J had plans to bounce back from the throat shot and sting the girl in the face with a swift swing. Underestimating her may result in his capture. Almost immediately after he hit the boy, he could no longer move. His body is frozen stiff. No follow through. No triumphant retreat. All that is managed is an unexpected defeat.

At least the boy on the ground wasn't able to avoid his onslaught. He is lying on the ground spitting up blood as his companion rubs his back.

"Damn!" J can't believe he has been caught again.

The girl looks at him as if she were responding to J's obscene language. "You're nuts! Why'd you have to do that? You don't even know us! We could have hung you dead if we wanted to! How could you do this?" She begins wiping blood from the boy's mouth like a mother cleaning a child's face.

Suddenly, she comes face to face with J. She pulls back her arm and clenches her fist.

Time seemed to slow as J waited for the blow to land. J could do nothing as she wound up her free cheap shot. Contact is predictable. J figures his nose will take most of the blow. He sees her once possibly innocent face convert into a swarm of anger... hungry to attack. J can feel his own eyes grow larger as he knows what is coming. He can't move. He tries and retries. Nothing is moving. Slow motion follows thoughts of regret and wishing he could take back lost time. Maybe talking to them would have been the better way out.

It happens.

She makes contact.

No broken nose.

She didn't even hit his face. He was sure she would hit him there. She drops to her knee and plunges her fist into his diaphragm. The capsule of air behind his rib cage gives way to the retreat of whatever air was in there and J can finally move.

He falls to the ground and clutches his chest. He fights to take grasp of whatever air might be within reach of his lungs. Nothing. It has all left. "Deep breath. Deep breath. Inhale. Exhale. Come on." Nothing. The feeling of passing out seems unavoidable. Yet, somehow, he manages to begin breathing again. Slowly, air begins to re-enter.

"We are here to help you." She sits down next to him. "We know exactly who you are and what you have done. Attacking the government is by far, one of the best things any of us could have done. Only, you're the one that did it. We know why and from whom you are running." She grabs J's arm and makes an effort to help him up. "My name is Angel, and my friend, your victim, is Scott."

Scott nods reassuringly and massages his throat trying to rub out the still present pain in his air pipe. "Hey." His voice is scratchy. He knows the sting is going to be present for a while.

"Just about the only thing we don't know is why you are here. They usually don't drop killers into this area. When they do, they're here to kill us. We often have to save the lives of pathetic wannabes who haven't the slightest idea of what type of lives we live in the zone." Angel points directly at J when she says killer. "You killed a lot of people boy. A lot more want you dead. Few want to see you alive. At least that's what we want them to keep fishing for. Your stunt was beautiful. Only the ignorant would be so arrogant as to think you intended to kill innocent people."

"It wasn't our fault." Now able to take a full breath, he could say something. It felt like an eternity since he was able to move and even longer since he had been able to inhale fresh breath. "We held meetings! They knew when, why, and how it was all supposed to happen. They helped…"

"You mean that there was more to that display than just yourself?"

"Yeah, there…."

"I knew it!" Scott interrupts. "I knew there was no way some dumb kid could do all that damage by himself. No offense kid."

"I don't know about that." J is caught speaking before thinking. Who are these people? What do they want? "If you two don't mind, I have to leave now. They are coming." He staggers past the two and heads for the front door.

"You're not going anywhere, kid. You don't know where you are or even who we are. How can you possibly expect to be able to defend yourself against odds of which you have no idea?" Scott beats him to the door. "After I take a blow like this from you, I am not just going to sit back and let you be prey to whatever decides to make you its meal. I'm gonna get first dibs on you." He raises his arm and acts as if to take action on his words. But, instead, he places it on J's shoulder. "You, come with us."

It isn't long before they get J back to their small city. What the government has decreed as dead zones, unfit for habitation, these people are calling home. It seems to be functioning without the technological advances on which the rest of the world appears to be so dependant. This society, at first glance, seems to be a step back from the modern advances. There aren't any active spy scans asking you to submit your eye for ID or fingerprints being taken for admission to buildings. People aren't zooming the streets in vehicles and running down pedestrians. The dreadful monotonous look of city life doesn't wear its mask here. These people seem much better off not having to worry about what they do or where the next raid is going to come from. This is definitely the most perfect pre-Madaggan city that J could have ever seen or imagined.

Zone 6 doesn't have many tall buildings. None are taller than most of the trees surrounding the area. Towers have been constructed here so that the zone can protect itself from the intrusions of outsiders. People had come from neighboring territories to help rebuild after the war. The citizens of Zone 6 are some of those who had also been tossed out, by their Big Brother.

To J, the towers reminded him of stories about a time when they were used as tools of family warfare and futile attempt of controlling the city. Members of society would work for the strongest family so that they would be protected within the city walls by the towers. Those times were different, hundreds of years ago, but not too far removed from the way people are living here. Outsiders could ruin the entire organization. Fear forces these zoners to expect constant attacks. If the wrong person gets in, their entire existence will be jeopardized.

Scott explains that the people of the city run the towers. Government is not a problem in Zone 6. The citizens are responsible for protecting each other. If one member of the unit fails, the entire system will ultimately fail. No one person will ever be in control of the towers or any other method of defense arranged for this city. The entire zone has a code to which they are responsible. Each person must follow this code.

Put your lives in the hands of each other. If you cannot trust the person that you have given guardianship of your life, then you do not belong here. Everyone knows that the towers are there for their own protection. Not all outsiders are looking for a place to hide from the power of the government. Many of them are like pirates roaming throughout the country, avoiding Big Brother, and pillaging the zones that haven't set up their own defenses already. Others are simply working both sides of the law for their own selfish desires.

"You see, J, in Zone 6 we strive for harmony within our society. We've come to realize that there will never be a true Utopia, but we can live comfortably within the walls of this city. We don't have to worry about outside interventions as long as our protections hold." The three of them are sitting in the middle of a plaza where water runs into a fountain from a spring. Near the top of the fountain, a stone frog spits water at a fly made of stone. "Yet, our way of life continues to be threatened by a menacing enemy breathing down our necks. They are continuously threatening to destroy our peace. If they would just stay out, we would be fine. If they would allow us to live on and ignore our existence, we wouldn't have to rebel."

"How are they threatening you? They don't even know these places exist anymore. These areas are supposed to be so contaminated that life cannot flourish." As J says these words, he knows he shouldn't. Who would be so stupid as to believe that the government wouldn't know these guys are out here? *Secrecy is key, J.*

"Come on. You can't tell me you actually believe in the junk those schools have pushed into your brain. That's only what they want you to believe. If the city tells civilization that we can't exist, then they can eliminate us whenever they want. It relieves any pressure they have to deal with if everyone knew we were out here. This is also sort of where you come into play."

"Me? How?" Before today, J had always dreamed about people being able to start over and scrap the old ways. From what his grandfather had taught him, J knew that the government had too much control over its minions. Eventually, the minions will rise and destroy its master. Currently, there isn't much that the people can do. They don't have the power or the artillery to be able to confront the opposition. The government has a monopoly on the big guns.

"The country, as you know it, doesn't exist." Angel hands a small pocket book over to J. "You know the texts. You know that Madaggan led this country into its deadliest war ever. Of course, they will never publicize it as such. You know that people used to fear nuclear wars. They obviously have good enough reason to. The whole system has built you up to believe that there could be no life where the bombs hit. They want you to fear the fall out areas. They don't want people roaming wherever they see fit. The more expanded the country, the harder it is to control. You can't tell me that you never once thought that Madaggan, himself, had aimed some of those bombs at his own country."

"Conserve the fuel. Wait for them to run out of resources." Scott sarcastically quotes Madaggan's theories on how to take out the enemy. "If we conserved all that fuel and waited until they had burned most of their resources, how could we be attacked? How could they have had enough to fuel their own missiles? If our neighbors didn't hit us, then we hit ourselves."

J knows the stories. He can recall reading about Madaggan and how he was one of the greatest Generals of all time. Of course, his grandfather would passionately oppose all of this. *Madaggan was a tyrant willing and ready to destroy his own people for power.* The schools always contradicted grandfather, of course. They would push how Madaggan pulled the states out of a recession and made it so that public favor was placed back onto the system. At the height of his influence, he protected the nation from a seemingly unpreventable war with Canada. On the other hand, J knows that the zones were created because of Madaggan's War. He knew that it could have been avoided, but when the General acted too slowly, he doomed the rest of the nation.

Maybe he didn't act too slowly. It's possible that he meant to destroy his own people. No one knows who the first to act was. No one knows who won. Are we the only ones to survive this conflict? Who would be so arrogant to believe that there aren't others out there?

His actions created our way of life. Despite what the system wants people to believe, he was definitely the one speaking about the destruction of dynasties. He was the one pointing fingers at the world for holding back on goods and resources.

"How am I a factor here?" J poses this question to his new friends, if indeed you could call them that. How could he be of any use? How could people be so trusting? Something, in the back of his mind, continues to probe at the idea that he shouldn't be here. Yet, they think he can do something for them.

"The Government is beginning to exert more pressure on us. They probe these parts continuously. Every moment of every day, we have to have our eyes on them. If they would simply leave us alone, we would be fine. Unfortunately, we've come to realize they won't allow that to happen." Angel looks at Scott for reassurance. How much should they be telling him?

Scott catches the hint. "In order to prevent them from taking away our freedoms, which we enjoy so much, we send out our seeds. The seeds do something so outrageous that the rest of the non-accessible world knows we are still here. Usually, they assassinate a political figure or blow up a capital building. This may seem to be an act of terrorism, but is it such when we are being threatened for trying to live our lives without their interruptions?"

"What does this have to do with me?" The babbling is beginning to get to J. "I am not one of your seeds. I've done nothing for you."

"Of course you're not. That's the problem. You've done everything we are known to do. Now they have someone else to go after. Or, they'll choose to come here because of you. Since we are the closest zone."

"You were never a seed." Angel looks him in the face. "That's why you are so important to us right now. The little book… it explains everything. We believe that you are the one that is going to pull the people out of this mess. You are The Chosen. Do you understand?"

"The Chosen?" The words spill from his lips as if sacred and powerful. Yet, he can't believe he had just heard them spoken and then, spoke them himself. "Grandfather told me that some day someone would rise. He had been talking about that person just before the raid. I am not that someone. You cannot honestly think that I am."

"We need someone like you. We don't think that you are ordained by some supernatural being. We're not expecting you, J, to become god-like and throw your arm down to destroy the government. That's not what we believe." Scott and Angel look at J as if they are waiting for the kid to accept an open invitation to a neighborhood barbecue. "You are important to our cause. We believe that only you will be able to help us finally pull this off by inspiring the Zones to rise now. With the spark of an individual that is willing to act on his own, you are the person who begins our time bomb. Even if you don't believe you are who we are trying to say you are, you have to play the person. We depend on you to simply play the role. Everything else will fall into place. This is essential to get things moving now!"

"Why? I am not the person you think I am. When Grandpa foretold that someone would rise, I am sure he was not talking about me. I am just a simple kid who happens to have played a part in something that's bringing me to your attention. There was no individual. Grandpa and I planned it together." J sees no reason to fall back into discussing the event. The death of so many people is heart breaking. Especially, when it wasn't supposed to go that way. "Now, you want me to lie because you want people to think I am someone that I can't possibly be. It's ridiculous. I am no leader."

"You can think of yourself as just a kid. You have already made a powerful impression upon the world as one who will not be silenced. You have to gain the confidence to believe that you could possibly be the hand that sets everything into motion. They... fear you." The two of them gaze so intensely at J that he is reminded of children on

Christmas morning. Excitement on the verge of disappointment brightly paints itself across their faces.

"How am I a voice? I have said nothing to anybody. I have nothing *to* say. How could I be known throughout the world? We don't have that type of technology. Nobody has been able to talk to the rest of the world since that war."

"More fragments of lies that they want you to believe. Do you not remember the bomb we've been talking about almost the entire time you have known us? You set it off a little less than a year ago?"

"You're insane!" A year ago seems like much longer than J can remember. It should have happened last week, maybe last month. How could a year have possibly gone by? Where has he been all of this time?

"Do you remember much after you set your plan in motion? Where have they had you all this time?"

J wants to say yes. He wants to stress that it hasn't been that long.

Yet, his memory isn't allowing him to remember the events in between his capture and the night that he woke up in that wet atmosphere. There is a black hole in his memory absorbing all of the events between that explosion and today. Can he claim temporary memory loss? Is it believable? Is he himself, or has he been removed from himself? Maybe he became a subject to the government itself where they sent him out to do their dirty work. When they found out they couldn't keep drugging his memory, they decided to allow him to wake up from whatever he had been dreaming. Who knows?

"I was caught, knocked out, and here I am." Is there really anything else? Possibly. Has it been as long as they say?

"They must have drugged you good. You made world news. You put Big Brother into complete chaos.

They couldn't believe that a kid like you put such a hurt on the system." Angel speaks with excitement on her tongue. "Compared to them, you are an insect that just happened to get into the works. Then you flubbed up the whole known colony. It is, because of you, that our seeds were able to grow. We know..."

"We know that you aren't the only one that was operating on that day. Fortunately, you didn't know this. Unfortunately, we didn't know what you were doing. It could have been better... more destructive. We had our own operations working that night too. We were lucky to have you do what you did. When your ticker went off, we were able to push ahead and take care of most of the rest of the city. We assassinated the President and they gave you credit for it. That was ingenious! They had no idea we were involved!" Scott put a hand on J's shoulder and lightly pushes it.

"The world thinks I killed the President?!"

"Yup, Chaz flipped when he heard you got credit for his assigned kill."

J knew his grandfather had planned to make a big impact on the system. He never knew it would be this big. He didn't even care to think about the assassination of the President. His death wasn't a part of the plan. What would that prove, anyhow?

Grandfather had wanted to shut down the system. He had everything planned out. They never knew what was happening. When the tunnels blew and left its mark on the city, anybody hit by it would not have felt a thing. Planned perfection. Yet, here J stands a year later. Was it really that long? J's confusion and uncertainty almost made a death sentence a welcome invitation.

"Your plunge had opened up such a vast field for attack." Scott's eyes are wide with excitement. His voice is ringing high with joy. "We may have had no idea that you were going to do it, but one of the buildings you took out, held the majority of the communication controls that they had up and running. When we saw this, we attacked too. We couldn't go for long, but we were able to add to what had already been ripped down. We hit them fast enough to hack all of their systems with Toad's bug."

"Calm down, Scott. He doesn't need to know it all right now. Telling too much more, might hurt us." J could see that Angel was also as excited as Scott, but she seemed a bit wary of J as well. Still she knew that this day had been a glorious day. She was glad to see that the easy attack had not been blown. Every opportunity given had to be taken. Everyday, they waited for something like this. Yet, Scott did not need to let the kid know anymore than the obvious. Even though they needed him, they really couldn't trust him just yet.

"You must join us. We want what every human be-ing must have. We want to live on in peace, but we have to continue to divert any attempt made to find us." Angel pauses, thinking over how to politely put across the idea that she does not yet trust him. "We want you to help us, but if you aren't who we think you are, or you don't play along, we will have to flush you from the network as fast as possible. We will not allow ourselves to be discovered."

"How long have I been gone? I don't remember much from the time after I was caught." J is massaging his temples still making a fruitless attempt to figure out why what he had done was so important and how he is supposed to play the role. "I don't even know what today is. Monday? Tuesday? Friday? I'm trying to process everything you two are throwing at me, but I just can't seem to make any sense of it."

"You've been out of the spotlight for a year. Yeah, of course people still talk about that wicked explosion, but it's been quite a while since anyone has publicly mentioned the event."

"We figure they're waiting for something to happen. Or they plan on making something happen."

That's how the system works everything to its own advantage. They display the event so long as people aren't going to be negatively impacted by it. They might run a few shows on the event, so that they can give the public good enough reason to make you a marked man, then they get rid of the evidence. Mention your crime publicly and you could be their next target. The channels won't say anything for any period of time beyond what the government wants them to. If they do, they get shut down. Raising discussion, on any outlawed events, may lead to the eventual overthrow of the system. Even with the President gone, everything is expected to flow smoothly on to the next day. Don't talk. They are listening.

Suddenly, a wailing sound bursts out in the distance. The ear splitting alarm echoes as if it is coming from the far end of the town. The people that had been walking peacefully throughout the plaza calmly vacate the area and disappear. Scott, Angel, and J are alone in the plaza. One would not have known anyone had been there. The evacuation was bizarrely calm and efficient. Scott and Angel pull J to his feet and, without a word, convince him that they too needed to find a safer place to be. A few seconds later, they are trotting down some side alley between two brick buildings which appear old enough to belong on the pages of a history book.

"Come on, kid!"

Halfway to the end of this narrow street, Angel kneels down and removes a hole cover. A spot, just small enough to allow them to slide through, becomes exposed. Quietly, she slides herself down into the black abyss and nothing could be heard from her touching the ground beneath. The darkness swallows her small frame and she vanishes as if she were never there.

"Go!" Scott nudges J from behind. Instead of going forward, he backs up. Jumping into what he cannot see does not strike him as the intelligent thing to do.

"Come on!" Finally, a voice comes from beneath. Angel has made it. Even if he couldn't see the bottom, he could at least tell that someone was down there waiting.

J stands, frozen, wondering what everyone has to run from. You don't have to hide in a 'Utopia'. Do you? "Why are we running?" Are they coming for him?

"You ask too many questions, and at inopportune times! I'll explain later. Go!" This time Scott pushes him forward and makes sure that J gets through the hole. He falls through the twilight where Angel had just previously descended. As J feels the reassurance of the floor beneath his feet, Scott immediately follows. He turns and closes the hole behind him as he stands on an old crate to help him reach it. "We can't take any chances here."

Some how, Angel manages to get a strand of lights working in the hallway. J hadn't noticed any switches that she may have triggered to get the stream of lights on. Scott nudges J and he gets the idea. He is supposed to move forward. Forward and away from whatever is behind them.

"What's going on guys? Why are we running?"

"Keep going. We'll explain later!" Scott pulls on a hidden lever as they are closing in on the end of the hall. Instantly, the stone wall in front of them slides open and another slides closed at their backs.

The hole or path or trail or wherever they are, looks like the typical underground sewage system. J wonders if an alligator might meet them around the next bend and eat them whole. Darkness is broken only by the occasional light bulb hanging from the ceiling. The light's weak glow exposes bits of whatever masonry-like talent had been put together in developing this underground escape route. Wasn't really much to it. It all appears to be simply laid out by 10-pound bricks. These bricks built upon themselves to form the walls. Patches of mud can be seen in places where water might have run through at one time or another. J and his grandfather had done a better job on the chamber of explosives than this. He quickly pushes this thought from his mind. It was too painful to reminisce.

This structure was either too old or too weak to be used for any purpose beyond escape. Even that might be a hard role to play anymore. This can easily be seen. Water falls from the roof of this rabbit hole and cascades down to the ground beneath their feet. J wonders if they were moving under a lake or river. He then nervously wonders how long this ceiling will hold together. Crevices and cracks had been born wherever the water dripped. Puddles of water lie throughout the entire network of tunnels before and after them. If they stood still and the sirens were not running, J bet that they could hear the water echoing like footsteps on marble floors. J's ears ring due to the noise and he longed for that silence.

The passage seems to continue on forever. J tries counting each step for each turn they make so that he might be able to find his way out if he needs to. If the tunnels collapse and his guides were to be crushed, he would need to know how to escape. There were so many steps and so many turns that he lost count. Maybe the person who created this maze, never wanted the Minotaur to ever get out. The sameness of the tunnel at each turn starts hurting his eyes. His mind is going crazy. The thoughts in his brain trying to outrun his feet.

Each trail leads down deeper into the never-ending labyrinth. Yet, there are no dead ends and no quizzes to be answered. No Minotaur waits for them at the beginning of any path. They keep moving, running faster with each turn.

Scott and Angel seem to know exactly where the danger lies and thankfully aren't willing to lead J into its deadly grip. As ill built as the passage could be, the maze would be hard to conquer if one had not traveled these trails many times before.

They say that J is important to their "cause." He feels like an endangered species being protected by a mob of conservationists. This time, there are only two people in the mob. Unfortunately, J feels, they are wasting their efforts. He couldn't be this person that they are waiting for.

"Who are we running from?"

"Shh. You'll know soon enough," Angel whispers to him as she tilts her head from next to him.

Suddenly, the deafening shriek of the siren now rings throughout the tunnels with continuous echoes of high pitch sound. J cannot tell where the sound is coming from as it fills the tunnel. Painfully screeching in their ears and hard for all of them to bear, the sound pounds their skulls. In an attempt to muffle the sound, they cover their ears. Sound waves are blasting so loud that they can barely stand on their feet. Yet, somehow, they managed to go further. They continue to push on at a sluggish running pace. How long have they been running? Painful... Loud... J's mind is splitting from the extreme pitch. His thoughts, from earlier, have left him. He had enough of a struggle just holding his skull together.

Angel manages to grab his shirt, pull him close to her, and then thrust him into an unseen opening in the wall. Scott and she enter, both as pale as the whitest albino. A wall of mud laid masonry closed behind them. As it closes, the sound is diminished. What has been only 2-3 minutes of unbearable noise, feels like an eternity. Ringing still exists within the walls of his own mind.

J sticks his fingers in his ears and wiggles them around a little. Loudly he speaks, "I think I am deaf." He knows it's not possible to be so, he just needs to hear something other than that noise. He shakes his head. "You guys want to fill me in now?"

They look at each other for a long time, nod, and then focus their attention back on him. "Where do we start? The sirens, or, the Prophet?" They are also screaming to compensate for the ringing in their ears.

"The sirens warn us when someone is coming that we don't know about. Typically, we get a few buzzes from these outside renegades. Sort of like the groups we were talking about in the plaza. Recently, we've been getting a lot of hits from the military. This is what scares us the most." Angel wiggles her finger in her ear to relieve some of the ring.

"The Prophet, on the other hand, is the one man who predicted the fall of the government which we all used to swear our allegiance to. He spoke about the death of a leader and the overwhelming control of a mad man leading that nation into utter chaos. Take a look around you. He said that the leader would be slain and replaced by the closest person to him. President Scarvaw was not only murdered on television, but a life long friend killed him. You saw the pictures in the house. He was the little guy next to Madaggan. Almost immediately after he killed the President, the country swore their allegiance to him. Looking at history, no one can find proof that anyone even showed a fragment of sorrow for the death of Scarvaw. No one. The Prophet was right." Scott looks to Angel to tell her part.

"Text pads tell about how Scarvaw was going to overthrow the role that the government played in protecting the people. He was planning to strip them of their rights and begin fresh. They say that his radical ideas gave the people more than enough reason to want him out of office. When Madaggan answered their prayers, they accepted him with open arms. They said the man had made "a radical choice, and chose the right way to act." Angel scratches her palm. Somewhere along the path, she had somehow cut her hand.

"The Prophet then predicted that the country would easily fall under the control of this new Commander-in-Chief and a war would soon follow. He clearly stated that the war would be a nuclear one. This war would devastate the union of the country and split it against itself. During his life, the Prophet was sending out messages that nobody could believe. If only they were alive today. You can see it all the way you want. You are the one to interpret these events the way you believe them to be. We see it the way it is. The country is split and fighting itself. Hundreds of dead zones want to regain power of the country and the Big Guy wants us to stay out of the picture. Most of the dead zones do not support the way the system is currently running. We try to communicate with the rest of the world to let them know what we are going through. Yet, there are still areas of the country that believe the government is doing exactly what they need to do to keep the country functioning."

"Because we have been enlightened by his books, he is well known by many of us. We try to do what we can to educate those who are not a direct part of our community. He has helped us so much. It's a shame to see that he had been killed simply because he could see things that people did not want to believe in. Luckily, before he was eliminated, he was able to spread one more prophecy. The one theory many of us hold dear to ourselves. We search endlessly to the fulfillment of this event. He said the future would have a chosen person who would come and lead the oppressed into a new era. We only dream that this day might soon come." Angel's eyes have a hopeful gleam about them.

A dream fulfilled in J? J wonders if the people are so impatient to wait for the right person, this "Chosen One," that they throw in and abuse every person they feel the need to believe in. Is J a part of such a plot to fulfill an unpromising theory? Are they just looking for someone to "play the role'" so that they can find motivation behind their cause?

"A Democratic dictatorship is going to fall." Scott looks down at the ground. Angel places her hand on his shoulder and continues in Scott's stead. "We honestly believe... Our people have total faith that the chosen one is among us. This person will come out and leads us. We have hope. Hope that this person will someday feel the same frustration that we do. Maybe then... they may step forward. Until then, we will continue to punch the system whenever we can."

J slouches down. "Wow!" He is beginning to realize what they are talking about. All of his life, Grandfather had spoken of the chosen one. He never realized how universal this idea had become. He usually blew the man off as some crook. Then again, he never knew that the dead zones actually existed.

Even when they built that death trap, he never really took in how much of an impact that event might have on the government. "When we built the tunnels, Grandfather always talked about this guy. He had a bunch of ideas. I always thought that maybe he was my grandfather."

"Have I forgotten to mention how you guys did the best thing that could ever happen in the history of the zones?" Angel interrupts and startles J. "This is one of the reasons we think it's you!" Excitement rings in her voice. "You are going to help us bring them down. Even if you aren't him, it's important to act as if you are. You have already begun the process. Now, they're more paranoid than they have ever been. In an attempt to find us, they keep making mistakes that are going to cost them in the long run."

J isn't exactly sure how they can be thinking that the bomb gives them enough reason to think that he is the chosen one. Not in his wildest fantasies could he envision himself taking out the bad guys. Nor can he see himself being the person they want him to be. "Just play the role." There are too many of them. He is just one person. If they are expecting him to do what he has already done, he isn't confident that it can ever happen again. Taking other people's lives isn't exactly his dream of how to live his own.

The question of what they had been running from pops back into his mind. He knows they are running from the military, but he figures the army would have enough technology to be able to detect a town in chaos with sirens blaring and all. So, they would easily find the place and wipe them out. He is also wondering if the entire town has emptied into the labyrinth of halls. If they have, he hasn't seen anybody else since they had come below.

"We are almost there." Scott is referring to wherever they are heading. The same wall that served as a shelter from the mind splitting siren earlier, now opens into a new corridor of the maze.

J has just become comfortable sitting with his back to the opposite wall. He had become so relaxed he never realized the small chamber they were using to rest in was moving in any direction. He stands up, brushes himself off, and finds his way out of the shell and into a room of endless amounts of people. He can't see any wall here, except the one he just came through.

The roof was 40 feet high and lit up by lights, which seemed to bounce and respond to each other's energy. J could see stalactites dripping into bowls just above the lights. Each drip of fluid seems to fire and light the torch a little bit more every time. He is amazed at how these glowing bowls are capable of lighting up the rest of this enormous cavity.

The people, here, have somehow turned the insides of a cave into a booming district of business where they come together to barter and communicate. No wonder Big Brother can't reach out to claim these individuals. J can see all ages spreading themselves across the floors of this underground city. He swears he has seen some of them at his grandfather's speeches, but they show no sign of recognizing who he is.

Miniature structures have been constructed to look like an urban community. Buildings tower to the ceiling, but they are nowhere as large as the typical city buildings. Yet, it seems, that they are immersed in the city life. People can be seen disappearing into these buildings and coming out with every day items that they would have in their own homes. How could they shop for goods, which they were unable to obtain? How did they get the food, which they are unable to grow?

It seems that the network works without any trouble from the outside. The people seem to be calm as they travel from one place to another and converse with one another. Maybe these evacuations were something normal for them. Maybe this is a utopian community working in its best way.

In the center of this place, stands a statue of a man looking off into the distance. He holds a book in one hand with the pages facing down, and a staff in the other with a globe at the top. His stare reminds J of a person in thought. He seems to be looking at something off in the distance, but J can't tell if it is anything within the cave. Realizing that he has no idea where he is, he foregoes trying to figure out where the figure may be looking to. Motionless, it stands alone. Silently, it portrays an unexplainable something that J has never seen before. Few people are as admiring of it. Its presence already too routine on the minds of these people for them to take much notice. To pay too much attention to it, now, may be pointless.

At one time this statue was important. Maybe it still is. It's possible that there is more to the story of this village. Is he the founder of this underground society? Is he responsible for pulling all of these people together? What is his story?

XI

"Sir, He's gone."

"What do you mean?" Bzzt. The other side of the receiver isn't working up to code. The annoying bzzt has become so common that it is considered normal to begin talking after the buzzing sound.

"Our pickup is gone. He's out of range, sir." Bzzt. Even telling this to the General is a risk to his job. Being the bearer of bad news is never safe.

"Find him!" Bzzt.

"Yes, sir!" The young private, roughly 19, picks up his headset. He wraps the wire from one ear to the other and around in front of his mouth. Then, he begins talking into it. "The kid has escaped and the blood hound has lost his scent. Even worse, we've lost the hound. We are requesting any help that can be given."

The headset barks back. "We've got a location on your hound. He's been packaged and shipped. He's in Capital City. Do you want a forward on his signal? Or, would you like us to chase it down?"

"Retrieve the hound and bring him home." The private ends communication with the satellite station and clicks over to the General. "Sir, one of our branches is stating that they have a reading on our man and he is in Capital City. He has been packaged. I can't believe they've done it again." Bzzt.

"Packaged!" Bzzt. A second of silence crosses over the airwaves. "Not again! Is this one still alive, Private?" Bzzt. Many of their trainees have been captured and killed. The last month has seen at least 20 individuals eliminated while doing a simple pick up. The anti-government scabs have been rising and becoming more daring. This is consistently making it harder for the Internal Affairs to hire anyone who might be willing to dare the risk of capture. Even with higher pay and a promise of political power, fear of death holds far more persuasion than any incentives.

This is the third package shipped from the eastern coastal dead zones. Fortunately, it proves that someone is out there. Someone is calling for an invasion. The question is when.

"Sector C, do you copy?"

"Go ahead, X."

"Is our dog alive?"

"Yes, sir. Your dog is alive and well. This one got lucky. The fox wasn't hungry."

"Sir, he's alive." The private relays the message to the General.

"Good! Send some men to Capital City to retrieve the dog and get a second group out to where they last had a trace of him. We need to cut down the scum that keep doing this to us. If we don't put some hurt on them now, they won't let us operate as easily any more. Find them! Kill them! I don't care if they are little children with lollipops! I want them dead!" Bzzt. The vibration of his voice echoes off the walls of the private's relay room. "And do something about this goddamn annoying buzzing sound!"

"Consider it already done, sir." The earlier approval, to retrieve the hound, is an order that should have been waited on. As long as it seems like it is the General's idea, everything is safe. If the General knew that he had already made the command without his orders, he would spend the next twenty years of his life in a prison cell wishing he were dead.

"Are we done here Private?!" Bzzt.

"Sending out locations and commands as we speak." The private loves this part of the job most of all. This is the main reason he joined the Internal Affairs, went to all those boring classes, and works these crappy endless hours. Not much of a life for him outside of this place. Here he can sit in front of a large holographic map and dictate, as if he were any commanding officer, to his peers. Here his directions are their commands and other's orders. To disobey would be to ignore an order from a higher commander.

"PCBI, your orders are as follows. I am sending all information to you via hologram chips." He touches the glass screen that displays all of the data he needs to send out. A small clear chip falls from the right hand corner of the screen, and he plugs the chip into the side of the map projector. This map lights up and a transparent blue wall forms around the edges of the receiver. The machine begins buzzing and he knows that the operation is under way.

They are fast to act. As soon as the machine before him is ready to go, a group of six Day Stalkers are sent out from a base closest to the given destination. The Day Stalkers are considered an extravagant piece of machinery. They are built with the capability of flying, floating, and/or driving in any conditions. All of this can be done while remaining completely naked to the human eye. These strengths make the Day Stalkers one of the greatest military inventions of all time. Also, as small as they are, they are capable of carrying 20 men in and out of a battlefield with ease. Plainly, this vehicle makes it so that surprise attacks anywhere, would and could be fatal. Seeing the ships on their way and knowing their abilities, the private smirks and laughs.

"Coordinates received, mother bird." What he wouldn't give to be able to fly one of those. Unfortunately, his rank isn't high enough.

The private watches as the flock of freshly flying Stalkers cut through the air on their way to their destination.

From the holograph, he can easily see the 3-d models of the aircrafts gliding swiftly through space. He can examine any miniscule changes in the landforms, weather, or even the craft itself. If there are any contaminants in the air, he could pick them out and name each one. Anything he wants to know about the area surrounding and within the Day Stalkers, he could get as long as he is linked with them.

Soon he would have to cut the link. Afterwards, they will continue communicating through headsets. Remaining linked to the Stalkers for too long would open up waves for hackers to crawl into. If they get onto the waves, they have access to everything he can do. They would be able to find out enough information to nullify the attack. Even though it has never been done before, the fear always remains. Any operator hopes that the viruses left on the waves will hold the hackers back long enough for the operator to at least be warned before the link is compromised.

From the ground, no one is able to see these crafts. They may be able to feel the breeze of the whole flock as it zips through the air, just skimming the treetops, but it is easily passed off as a gentle breeze.

Yet, the private muses, there isn't supposed to be anyone in the area where they are heading. It had been stricken as uninhabitable because of Madaggan's War. If anyone is found, they will simply be terminated. That is the way to deal with the non-existent. People are led to believe the war had ended up destroying much of the life that had once thrived here.

It is still shocking that the trees managed to grow back as quickly as they did. Maybe they never disappeared. Chemical bombs had decimated most of these areas so many years ago. That's what the system wants you to know. That's what most of the honest citizens believe. Yet, people are living out here. Still, the pilots of the Stalkers should be able to fly undetected.

There wasn't any real justification for the extra 120 men loaded onto the Stalkers. The unexpected, however, always seems to happen when you're not prepared. They can't afford any mishaps, especially after the events of this last year. The mission must be completely successful. They bring the men along to guarantee success. Take no prisoners.

The pilots understand that the mission is as easy as simply landing, just out of range, unloading the men, and flying off undetected. What happens at that point is a result of specialized training. Execute, as commanded, and leave no trace behind. No one should know we exist.

The private gives a jolt as he notices something on his hologram. "PCBI, you are being scanned. Sirens have sounded to the South of your current location. Are you visible?"

This is impossible. Nobody has the technology to scan the Stalkers without being noticed ahead of time. This can't be happening. No way…

"We've reached our given coordinates. We're aware of the sirens. Do you want us to land or engage the source that seems to be tracking us?" Hovering, the pilot leading the voyage looks out over the spread of trees and mountains. With all of these trees here, the pilot wonders if there are actually people living out here after the prolonged period of radiation had kept them away. It is possible. He knows there has been many before. As the pilot continues to gaze down at the green landscape, he wonders what is tracking them? How could anything be tracking these birds? With the technology wrapped up in these things, it is virtually impossible to do so.

"Proceed into the designated area with caution. Maybe we have a lead on something."

"Roger." He pushes the controls forward and the Stalker moves swiftly toward the sounds of the sirens. When they arrive, nothing can be seen. Treetops protect the ground for as far as the eye can see. Nothing appears different from anything they have seen before. Everything seems to look just as it should, which makes the pilot nervous.

"Anybody see anything?" The commanding pilot is slightly confused. The sound and vibrations given off from the sirens are so close; they have to be sitting right on top of it. Yet, they can't see a damn thing. The mere force of their engines should have been enough to disturb the foliage enough to see at least patches of the forest floor below. Strangely, the trees are suspiciously still.

"No, sir."

"No, sir."

"Only trees, sir. Want us to take them down? Moving the trees will give us sight, sir."

"We need a clearing first, Maczendewski. We need an open field. Can't go firing on something we can't see. This could be a trap. Shoot into it and we could all go up in flames."

Without warning, a giant lead ball streaks through the trees and crashes into one of the Stalkers. It shouldn't have done much damage, except directly after that one, many more were on their way. One of the unsuspected balls plugged a rear jet engine from one of the flyers. It instantly explodes and takes off the back half of the Stalker. The vehicle spins out of control and crashes into the trees below. None of the men inside had a chance to escape. They weren't aware of the attack on their Stalker until it was too late. As it hit the ground, the fuel reserve combusts and kills any survivors.

"What the Hell?!" Roy sees the chaos of lead balls zipping through the air as he spins his Stalker towards the ambush. Each consecutive shot is making contact with one craft or another. Each Stalker as confused as the last. "Remain steady and get out of the air."

Even though the Day Stalker is one of the most high tech military vehicles of the age, every pilot knows that it is not a fighting vessel. Its primary usage is dropping off land troops and making a series of readings throughout the areas where it either has been or currently is. Stealth is its strong suit, not combat. Sometimes, it would even be responsible for leaving viruses, wiping out a region of life, then leaving ground troops to come in and clean up the mess. Get there fast, drop the troops, and get out. Be quick and be quiet.

Today's mission isn't supposed to be anything like this. They aren't supposed to have to worry about some freakish onslaught. They have been in cloak mode. They have been undetectable.

The second claimed bird falls from the sky like a duck over a pond during hunting season. It spins out of control until it finally makes contact with one of the trees. It instantly becomes engulfed in flames. Soldiers cry out in pain as they burn inside their tomb. No one moves to save them. They are gone already.

"Two down!"

"Keep firing! They don't know who, where, or what we are." Mike Parks begins laughing at the top of his lungs. "We've got 'em! Don't spare the ammunition! We won't be taking any of it with us."

"Fire!" These words can be heard, by all, standing on the ground looking up towards their invisible targets. No one can see the Stalker fall from the sky until it is actually hit by one of the cannon balls. When the ball hits, it spread a pulse of energy throughout the cloaked bird and begins to eat away at the armor of the ship. There are no plans to recover the technology. They only want to destroy it.

"We'll never give them our freedom! They'll have to kill us all!" Mike holds a small piece of glass in front of his face. "B8! J1! To the last man boys and girls."

"Hit! Hit!" Who would have ever known that the idea of 'Battle Ship' could work in the sky? With the heat sensors set at the top of the trees, a grid-like format can be used to detect where each of the invaders are.

"Yes! Haha! They don't have the slightest idea!"

The glass acts as a grid. The grid reads the presence of something in the sky above and around the town. Then, it sends a message to an eyeglass hanging around the heads of the assailants. From the grid, Mike and his group can see where they need to aim their cannons. In a state of alert, each person has to cooperate and be as accurate as possible. A miss could mean a life. If the grid is destroyed, the game is over.

The hologram of trees stands strong and flawless in this time of desperation. The aircrafts can't see through the trees, and it isn't hard for the ground crew to be able to tell which of the trees are real. If they hit any of the real trees, they chance hitting a hologram projector and throwing off their location. Knocking out the projector will put a glitch in the connection between the grid and the fake forest protecting them. A single clip through one of them could knock out all image projection capabilities that are needed at this precise moment.

"Take these guys out!"

In the skies, chaos and panic are rampant. "Flee! Retreat! We need to land these things!" Roy is losing control of the Stalkers. There doesn't appear to be a single steel magnet missing these birds. Each ball adds a dangerous blow to plucking another one from the sky. Each one that falls, putting more lives in danger.

Three of the Stalkers have been knocked from the air. That's three more than should have been allowed. That's possibly 60 men lost. Yet, they can't fight back. Once the rampage started, it was difficult to see where our allies were and impossible to see his assailants. Even if they could have seen their attackers, the Stalkers aren't built to repel enemy fire. If they can't get to the ground, then the mission is over.

The sirens, from below, have stopped sounding. Whatever warning that was deployed is no longer there. They must think they have won this battle. Maybe they are too confident in themselves. Three Stalkers in the sky means at least sixty men to put on the ground. When they are able to land, they become an unforgiving force.

"They'll be back! Keep all eyes open and all defenses up. We cannot allow these guys to get past us. The village depends on our stand here."

"Village is clear, Mike." Cheetah rejoins the group. "All of the residents are in the mountain. Shall we be going too?" She stands patiently awaiting an answer or an order. She knows her job. If he says, "Let's go," she will be responsible for controlling the hologram of the town and its surroundings. Then, she will be the last one into hiding. All entrances will have to be sealed. If he says, "We stay," she will hide behind one of the few real trees and wait for the next order.

Waiting to expel all of her energy, she would love to have the chance to rip one of those government issued soldiers apart. Maybe she would jab a knife into his armpit and tie it there so that the prey couldn't quickly remove it. While they fight to remove it, she would jam a knife in the throat of another oncoming enemy. Then, she would love to take on another in hand-to-hand combat. Toy with the individual, build up confidence, and take it away even faster. Finally, she would kill the first victim with the knife that might have been brought loose. All of this done, while maintaining enough balance and speed to stay alive and ahead of her enemies.

"Did anyone get hurt? Any villagers injured?"

"No. Nothing serious. Everyone was given enough warning to be able to evacuate at their own pace."

"Good. We can't have stunts like this putting them at risk. They depend on us to keep them safe. We do our job and they get to live another day."

Although the Zone lacks a singular leader, every individual in the community possesses a particular skill of which he or she has been assigned for an emergency. Each person has to do his or her part with the ultimate objective in mind. Stay out of the reach of Big Brother. Now, because of all that has happened, they are going to have to pack up and move again. Back into the mountain and onto another dead zone. Hopefully they can locate one that has been overlooked by the government, and isn't already occupied by another group of zoners.

"Okay, Cheetah. Let's get out of here. They're gonna be coming fast and we need to be moving even faster. You know what to do."

"I understand!" She is excited, yet sad. A chance to prove her strength and they have to move again. A chance for a kill and the dice refuse to roll her way. She wished she could stick around long enough to fight, but the colony depends on her.

"PCBI to head quarters..." Roy calls in to let Private Corvo know of their status. Even though the HQ had topnotch equipment working to their advantage, they never used it to keep an eye on their units for too long. This is common practice. Only when it is absolutely necessary, should a pilot contact the headquarters.

"Go ahead, Roy." The voice of Corvo springs back through the connection.

"We've suffered casualties."

"What?!"

"We've suffered…."

"Casualties! Yeah! I heard that part! How in God's name could this have happened?"

"We were ambushed from the ground through a bunch of trees. We couldn't see them."

"Get in there and take that center out."

"We're on it! I can't believe they saw us coming! It's like we are being attacked by ghosts."

"You realize that you can't come back without doing just that." Roy didn't need to be reminded. Either you die at work or in the office. A failure like this would guarantee his immediate elimination. Being the Commander of such important machines holds enormous responsibility. Losing them is not an option. If the technology gets into the wrong hands, it would destroy all that they have been working to stop.

The Stalkers are directed to land a half mile north of where they had been ambushed. All of them had badly damaged exteriors. None were sure if the damage would prevent any transformations. Yet, at least when they tried, it was successful. This was probably the most successful part of the day. Transforming from the sky, to a hovercraft is simple. No changes are made to the cargo or fuselage. The thrusters redirect themselves, from pointing to the rear of the vehicle, to pointing directly down. This allows them to float on the surface and jump to the sky as quick as needed.

The others quickly vanish into the mountains. Cheetah hangs back and bags her projector. After all, she can't let her baby be lost to the bad guys. She had developed this unit all on her own. "Another victorious day," she caresses the projector as it is tucked into her travel sack. She packs the machine tightly into her bag so that she can easily maneuver through the tasks to come.

Turning off the device reveals a previously hidden open field. Where the town's tower had been standing, trees become ever present. "Safe in the box." The buildings disappear and the field, before her, shows barely any hints of someone being there.

She moves quickly. It won't be long before the Stalkers are knocking at her back door. She has to seal off the entrances. Each entrance is rigged with a bundle of explosives and attached to cables that have been run underground for any upcoming situations such as this. As she is finishing her task, she sees the Stalkers approaching from the valley below. "We showed you." She picks up a stone and throws it. "Just like David and Goliath." Cautiously, the Stalkers pace forward.

"We are approaching the attack zone, sir."

The field in front of them appears to be abandoned. One could only see that something might have been there before they had arrived.

"Where are all of the damn trees?"

"Gone?"

"Why couldn't we just land right here?"

"Our sensors were reading solid mass beneath us, sir."

"Then, we can't be in the right spot! It's not possible!"

"We are, Roy."

"Then, you have to explain how there could be solid space in a place so empty."

"Not sure, sir."

"Scan the area. We need to find these guys. I can't believe they were able to do this. How can these zoners be capable of this?" The only possible explanation would be that they have technology more capable than their own. Without the facilities, how could they possibly produce such equipment?

"So long, peeps." Cheetah runs into the final hole and presses the ignition button on her wristwatch as she turns the first corner. A door slams shut behind her and a loud screeching sound begins echoing through the tunnel. This siren is a fair warning for those who may still be in the halls. Now, they are in danger if they are too close to the entrance or in any unstable pathways.

Outside, the explosion blows large slabs of stone away from the mountain's surface. This breaks loose the face of the mountain, causing a rockslide, which will cover any access to the tunnels within the range. Not only does it fill the necessary spaces, it also gets rid of any immediate threats. Boulders are literally flying through the air toward the Day Stalkers. The valley will soon be filled with rubble and they will never find their targets.

The men looking on from below have just enough time to begin praying. Jumping into the air would only propel them into the boulders quicker. Those in the cargo bay never knew what was on its way. Squashed, like a bug under the thumb of an angry bug hater, the machines buckle and cave in under the pressure of a thousand tons. If the men inside had not finished praying before they died, it wouldn't matter anymore.

XII

A mass of people, large enough to exist as its own town, survives within miles of rock. They wander about doing their own thing. Knowing that they are going to be here for awhile, they seem not at all troubled at their misfortunes. They have made their lives as comfortable, as can be, underground. They have even become so accustomed to their lives that they seem to be living better than those on the surface.

J wonders how long are they going to be down here? How often have they done this? The noise from the atmosphere around is drowned out into the background where the darkness lives. Sometimes the noise of the underground civilization is loud and sometimes soft, but never uncomfortable. These people live in harmony with one another. No apparent tension exists among the people. They seem to be functioning as they feel a society should.

J stands still, watching them. He has never seen anything like this. Only in school would he have seen so many people, in one place, going about their own business. Outside of these walls, citizens are not allowed to meet in large groups. There are even restrictions on how many people can be standing still in any given area. Create a line, in front of a store, and you are asked to move on. Too many people, in the store, and they would be forced to close. Yet, here, busy as they are, they remain polite and courteous. No one forces them to hurry about their day. No cameras pop up from the floor scanning for warrants.

Never do they seem to yell or punch. Never does one person bump another without an apology. It is unreal to be standing in the middle of such a united place. If he had not seen this himself, he would not have believed it. They remind him of a colony of ants, each knowing what his or her job is and stepping aside when it isn't his or her turn anymore. Hours have gone by, but it still feels like J has only been in this place for a short period of time. Absorbing everything that he can, it shocks and humbles him to see so many different people working together for what seems to be the common goal of living together peacefully.

In the distance, a bell begins ringing. It is nothing like the sirens from earlier. It is calm and relaxing, like the tone of a deep chime singing in the wind. In a calm manner, the people begin flocking to one end of the big hall. Some remain seated at the tables near the café where they are enjoying conversation and beverages. Others are leaning up against the buildings waiting for whatever the bell is introducing. Angel and Scott are no longer around. They too, are drawn to the center of the plaza. At least J assumes that is where they have gone. He doesn't remember them ever leaving his side or coming out of the shaft.

A large hologram, of an older man, develops on a raised platform at this end of the cave. He possesses a full face, dark eyes, and a negative appearance in his posture as if he is about to deliver bad news to the on looking crowd. He wears a business suit and is cleanly shaven. He is easily as old as J's grandfather had been. Yet, he must have been relatively important. All of these people are just waiting for the hologram to do something. J isn't even sure if the man knows he is being watched.

As his image grows clearer, the mild chatter disappears. Conversation ends and the people, who hadn't already been staring in his direction, redirect their attention. For a few long seconds, he says nothing as if he is challenging them to say something so that he can scold them for speaking out of turn. He smiles. At least it looks like he is attempting to break a smile through his cracked skin. It doesn't do much for his overall appearance. He speaks. It reminds J of what a turtle would sound like if it were carefully thinking through every word before it spoke it.

"You are meeting yet another brief inconvenience from our repressive system. We only hope that all of you made it here with ease. Sources have leaked that a group of Stalkers were, only moments ago, destroyed in your general area." He pauses. A small model of the Stalkers appears, in mid air, next to him.

The crowd screams in triumph. They didn't get to see the chaos that settled the conflict, but they knew they had been under attack by something. Boulders topple onto the vehicles and the image disappears. The people roar their approval.

The old man clears his throat and carries on. "I suggest that you do not surface within 20 miles of this area. They will be there soon. You will want to be on the move early tomorrow. Do not lose hope. The seeds for revolution are almost planted and soon all of the forgotten zones will be connected with one another. Soon, we will no longer be under this democratic dictatorship. Revolution is upon us? No! Revolution is upon them!"

The people cheer. "Victory! Victory!" They are loud enough to echo off the walls beyond the darkness. Everyone comes to their toes clapping. It is almost as loud as a mob of people cheering for their favorite team's win over a rival. Yet, as sudden as the cheer came, it died out. No one raises a finger to silence them. It was as if an applause sign blinked on and off too fast for J to see.

"We are waiting. You all have reason to believe that the Chosen One is among you. At least we hope that he is the Chosen One. Our cause lies on his shoulders. We all hope you were able to intercept him. He needs to know what his purpose is. You need to tell him."

He glances around to see if people are beginning to stare at him. They are not. J stands among them and begins to feel uncomfortable. If he is who they think, why can't they refer directly to him for their cause? He isn't truly who they want him to be. He was only asked to "play the role." J still hasn't agreed to help them. He has no wish of aiding them. He has already done too much. His part is finished.

The people remain hushed. No cheers. Silence. What are they thinking about?

J stands wondering what else this guy has to say and who on earth he is.

He has no idea that the people standing around him know exactly who he is. They think he is the one who should lead them in their revolution. They believe he would be able to break the system. He has already done it. Invincible… They don't know how, but this kid is going to do something that will unite the Zones under a banner of freedom. Maybe it's something he possesses. None of them know exactly what is going to happen or how this kid is going to help them. Each person has his or her own idea of what this Chosen One will do. Yet, no one can say for sure. What is the role of the Chosen One? Maybe he is there for the sole purpose of inspiration.

They all want him to go with their general plan. They all want him to allow the seeds to do their thing first. Then, they will put forth their assault. They will do it with or without him. With him, they seem to have a legit reason. Then, Big Brother will fall. Their success may depend on what this kid decides to do. Whatever it may or may not be.

The image, of the old man, flickers and blinks out of existence. For a few seconds, the people stand in remote silence.

From behind, Scott grabs J's shoulder. "Hey, kid, it's been a long day. We need to donate some time to the sand man."

J spins on his heals to face Scott. He is shocked and stunned as he pulls out of his stupor. "I was beginning to wonder when I would hear those words. Where do we sleep?"

As if to answer his question, the ground begins shaking with a low rumble beneath his feet. It echoes throughout the entire room. Suddenly, before his eyes, 100s of cots appear. Universally they are lined in rows and reach out beyond his sight. Next to each cot, a blanket is neatly folded into squares with small pillows resting on top.

J is awe stricken by this. "How did you do that?"

"I didn't. It's a part of daily routine. You don't think this is the first day we have been here, do you?"

XIII

Sleep overcomes J once again. Submission to the darkness is easy behind the doors of his eyes. A long day brings a person to an easy sleep. The cot isn't the most comfortable thing he has ever slept on. It is nothing compared to the genuine feather bed he slept on at his grandfather's.

However uncomfortable the cot may have been, J is immersed in dreams in a matter of seconds. Eyes shut, mind relaxed, heartbeat slows down, and subconscious begins to take over.

In his new world, he is looking down upon himself. A barricade of hospital equipment engulfs his body. His left leg has been opened to the left of his shin. Pin needles are holding the skin back like it would if he were a frog being dissected by a group of students. A mask is covering his mouth and nose. A tube leads from the mask to a steal pipe that is labeled, but the label can't be made out. J imagines that the bed is more comfortable than the cot he had been sleeping in at one time. That seems to be such a long time ago.

As he takes more time to admire himself, he notices that his body has been opened in a few more places, which he did not realize at first glance. He has tubes and wires hanging from almost every part of his body. People are drooping over him. They aren't doctors. At least, they aren't wearing the typical red uniforms. They aren't from the city.

In a flash of light, he becomes lost. Darkness closes in on consciousness. He feels like he is being stung by a colony of bees. Each stinger is continuing to inject itself into his body and leave a little something behind. The sensation spreads throughout his body. They are pinching, poking, and stabbing at his insides. They are traveling through his veins. He feels like he is going to explode. His blood is burning. His skin is boiling. He can't see anything. Maybe the pain has made him blind. Possibly, he is dead and this is Hell.

He wants to scream. He can't. He wants to run. His legs aren't moving. He isn't breathing on his own. He wants to pulls the bees out of and off of his body. He can't do this either. Something is restraining him. Cut loose! Break free! Run! They are coming! These invisible monsters won't leave.

Finally, he can open his eyes. He can see! The tubes, the machines, and the people intertwined with his body. They all appear to be a part of him... molded into his skin. None of them are familiar to him in the real world. Yet it all seems like an event he has endured before. Is this déjà vu? Is this just a figment of his dream world?

Pain!!! Storms of stinging sensations rip through his nerves!

"He's coming out!" A voice yells from above J, not at any particular person, but at the entire room.

"It's not planted! Put him back under!"

Darkness... Silence... Comfort... A cool numbing sensation fills his body. The pain slowly edges away from his nerves.

When he wakes again, he notices that the room has changed and the faces are even less familiar now than they were earlier. The arsenal of appendages once linked to his body, have been removed. He lay on his back staring up through a hole in the ceiling. Droplets of water are splashing down onto his face. Remembering what he thought he had just experienced and the pain he had briefly felt, he feels his body for scars, bumps, anything that might support the idea that something had been surgically implanted. Maybe he just wants to see if the dream had been a reality.

J is back in the wet cold room. The people aren't saying anything to him. They just look on and watch as he stares off into space. His numbed mind is racing to get no where.

Darkness.

"Go! Go! Go!" A man is screaming commands to a stampede of footsteps. "Our man is in there! Boys, you need him alive! Go!" J can hear the voice shouting, giving directions. He can feel the footsteps around him. The rumble of an organized pursuit is building up. Are they after him? Why? What do they want? What did he do? "If you kill him, the General will have your souls!"

Run! He can't. His legs are still frozen solid. The body is not able to move.

To his left, he hears a door burst open. The hinges splinter under the pressure. The plaster, hiding the steel frame of the door, spreads across the room. He thinks to himself that they didn't really need to break down his door. He never really locks it. They could have just turned the knob and everything would have been fine. The low rumble of feet slowly becomes louder. They have to be right on top of him. Why can't he look to see who is there? Why must he continue to stare at the sky? They are here, yet no one touches him.

A gun hammers in the distance. The slug pelts hard against something. The thud of the weapon is loud. J only hopes it wasn't somebody instead of a thing that was hit.

"Destroy! Anything that gets in our way! What do we do?"

"Destroy!" A unit, of men, echoes their answer.

"What is our main goal?"

"Capture and recover the target!"

"Call it a day, men!" The commander sends them to rest and the footsteps fade away.

"Where ever you are, we will be there. We will find and capture you. You are going to help us even more than what you expect, puke!"

Puke? What kind of word is that? Who is this man? How is J going to possibly help him? J would rather die than to have to hurt people again.

More pain. J can feel something sliding down his left leg. This time he can respond within limits. He opens his eyes and sees a few people huddled over his leg. He can't see what they are doing, but he can tell that they are definitely the cause of what he is feeling. His body is burning. He tries to move his arms and legs, but they are tied down. Within limits, he can move them enough to feel the uncomfortable tingle present where the straps are holding him down.

"I wouldn't move too much if I were you, kid." One of the men pop up and show him a wire thread that is covered in blood. "We just need to get this thing out of you."

What thing?

As if to answer his question that hasn't been spoken, the man goes back to work and begins mumbling to the others. At least J hears a few words. He made it out to be something about how they should have killed him. He was going to feel something, but it wouldn't be long, and something else about how he had almost gotten them all killed.

Pain…

He feels something pinching at the muscle in his calve area. He feels the vibration and hears the cutting of the bone in his leg. He screams. His body jerks in response to the pain. Not much else he could do. Not sure if he is feeling it, or if he is just reacting to that God awful noise and the Dr. Frankenstein-like atmosphere.

Pain!!!

"It's gonna be alright, kid. We're gonna fix ya all up."

"Why are you doing this to me?" He wants to scream out and protest the surgery, but his words are soft.

Pain!!!

"They've planted a tracer on you. We're removing it. Hold still best as you can."

"A what?"

Pain...

"Tracer... You know... If you want to follow or collect data on something without having to be within its sight, you plant something on it so that you can refer to it whenever you wish. A tracer."

He felt one of the men grind the blade into his leg again.

White lights burst behind his eyelids as immense pain floods his being.

He feels his leg being cut in half. He screams and jerks harder. Still can't break loose. They are on top of his leg, limiting his movement even more.

"Are you feeling this?" He heard one of them ask.

"Yes!" J responds through gritted teeth. How could he not be feeling this? Are they toying with him? Cutting him into tiny bite size pieces for some kind of sick cannibalistic meal? "How could I not be?" How could they not notice how much he had been jerking and tossing.

"Damn! Who didn't administer the right amount of drug?" The man went beyond his vision, made a little unrecognizable noise, came back, and stabbed him in the arm with a needle. "This'll numb ya up real good. Don't worry, when we're all done, you won't even know this happened."

Pain subsides and relief washes over him.

He is finally at ease again. Just as he could remember before he fell asleep on the cot. Any pain he had been feeling, is now gone. At least he thought he had been feeling it. Everything had happened so fast.

Darkness lingers for a short period. No dreams. No hospitals. No visions of people being surgically butchered. Before he could get enough rest, he is staring at the sky again. The cot lay beneath him and a full moon hovers above. He looks from side to side and notices the others also lying silently in their cots. How did he get outside? How did everyone get outside?

He bites himself. Ouch! He is awake. He feels his legs to see if the attachments are still there. No wires are present, just a bandage wrapped around his ankle. J wants to remove it and see what is underneath. When he pulls at it, his ankle responds with a stinging protest.

"Kinda hurts, huh?" The girl, who had been lying in the cot next to his, is watching him. Her dark hair lies lazily over her face covering one of her green eyes. It hangs there as if to tease you and dare you to see if the other eye is the same color. "I had one of those before."

"One of what?" He replied wondering, half heartedly, how long she had been actually watching him and why the bandage is there. It all seems like a dream. It was all a dream.

"A little device that sends your information out to the big guys." She smiles. Thin lips. Beautiful smile. "We sure are glad you talk in your sleep. If you hadn't we might not have known about this one. They would have surely killed us all. I only hope we got to it quick enough."

"Who would have killed us all?"

"What kind of question is that? Who else would want to put one of those things into a person?" She laughs either due to his ignorance or his innocence. "Of course, you know, now we have to move on and find another place where we are able to prepare traps to protect ourselves. It's just too risky to sit around and hope that they didn't or don't try to chase down their tracer." They were already going to have to move. This incident is just going to speed up the process.

"Tracer?"

"Are you really that lost? You don't even know what a tracer is?" She looks at him in disbelief. "They took a tracer out of your leg. It's one of the smallest ones we've seen out here. Mine was like a big black box that I couldn't take off without an extreme shock."

"You haven't answered my first question... Who?"

She thinks for a second. J could see her mixing her thoughts in her head. He couldn't believe she is even talking to him. In society, she would have never glanced in his direction. "The bad guys put that thing there. They, the government, seem to think that the outcasts of their system will just lead them into the homes of the enemy. It's not often that they actually make it here or anywhere else. There are very few of us who actually make it through. You are one of the lucky ones. What you did to them makes you one of the people that the village sees as a benefit to our community. Somehow, they seem to know this."

J looks beyond her to see if anyone else decided to wake. No one else is there.

"Nobody is sleeping. Like I told you, we have to find somewhere else to go. As soon as we heard about that tracer, we started moving out. Everyone had to get as far away from you as quick as possible. Very few of us hung back."

"How…"

"I'm sorry. Almost forgot to intro myself. I'm Cheetah." She throws her hand out in front of her, takes his hand from his lap, and shakes it. "I am in charge of holographics. Do you like this one?" She points up. The moon is still there. Stars are shining for as far as J can see. "We spend a lot of time underground. I figured something like this adds to the atmosphere. Besides, who doesn't like to sleep under the stars?"

"Nice." That's how he got outside. "Looks better than the real thing."

"I also created some of the city life atmosphere. Some of the people you saw were my own creation. Along with, of course, the buildings and general everyday doings of the events that people are expected to carry out."

"Really?" J envisioned some of the people he saw yesterday and wonders which ones were real and which were just fragments of her imagination.

"Hey!" Scott comes through a door in the near wall. He raises his right arm and waves it as if trying to get the attention of his friends who might be ignoring him. "We've got to pack up! Let's go!"

J looks around again. She said there wasn't any one sleeping. There didn't seem to be anyone in this place, either. The people, that had been lying there last night, were now gone. The cots are all deserted. Cheetah, Scott, and J were present in the room. That's it. "Where's Angel?"

"She is already gone. She had to move on with the rest."

"Move on?" J repeats these words as if this were the first time he had ever heard them come from his own mouth. His eyes glaze over and he stares off into nothingness. He can sense the presence of Scott and Cheetah, but his ears are blocking out whatever they are saying. Her mouth is moving, J doesn't comprehend.

"Move on." He restates them. His vision blanks out. It is hazy, blurred, and glossy all at the same time. He can see a group of men, in uniform, walking somewhere. Where are they? Who are they? Why is he seeing this? They are hurrying to wherever they are heading. Something is coming. Maybe even somebody is coming. He can sense that they are near and possibly looking for him.

XIV

Nothing. Emptiness. The holographic map's grids became empty. The Day Stalkers have disappeared. A line of communication ceases. How can this be? The Day Stalkers are undetectable. Yet, someone has spotted them. No warning appears in the grids before the squad is marked absent. They are pulled from the map like a screaming child in church.

Corvo reviews the data readings that had been recorded. The Day Stalkers were indeed cloaked. No changes in temperature. No hidden presence. Even heat vision fails to provide any clues. Not even as much as a bird flying under the troops. "What is out there?"

Private Corvo taps away at a few of the buttons on the screen of the hologram's glass surface. Nothing happens. The keys have forgotten how to respond to his fingertips. One hundred and twenty men can't be lost. He slams his fingers down onto the screen. Still, no response.

Checking for an electrical flow of energy, he flips open a hatch on the right side of the machine. An arrangement of lights continues to blink back at him. Wires cross each other and support the stream of power that this technology requires. The wires are intact and Corvo should be able to talk with the team. He fidgets with the controls one more time hoping that maybe this time he will get results.

Nothing...

"That's okay." He is trying to reason with himself and convince his own mind that everything is working to key. Even though technology is good and it is continuously being perfected, there are still random glitches in any piece of machinery. This time... He has to face the fact that it isn't the machine's fault or the fault of those who built it. This time it is beyond the machine. This time, it is unchangeable, untraceable, and uncontrollable.

He shuts the hatch and grasps the connection to the General. "We have a problem, sir." This is it. He can kiss his job goodbye. No way he is going to be here tomorrow.

The General listens as a few seconds of dead air replace the static like click of the receiver. Worry flushes through his mind. Frustration overcomes his eagerness for a response. "Private?"

"We have a problem, sir."

"I know." His voice comes through loud and clear. Whatever was jamming the frequency earlier isn't present any longer. The bzzt has gone.

"What do you mean?"

"Son, we know more than you will ever know, with or without your undependable technology. You're not the only one we get our information from." He pauses for a second and the silence in the air is menacing. "They are in hiding."

"Who?"

"Once again, we know things that you need not worry your pea sized brain over. Do you honestly think that the Stalkers are still out there trying to respond? Your dependence on tech scares me." He pauses. "What will you do when we don't have it anymore?"

A few minutes prior, when the Day Stalkers were no longer registering as operational, a few men had come into the General's office. They were all donning the same outfit. Kahki pants, white button up shirts, and oversized overcoats, which drooped to the ground picking up dust particles as they swept across the floor. The final touch of their attire was a dome shaped hat, which gives off the idea of an overturned soup bowl. None of them look fit for the military. Too frail to carry a weapon and defend themselves. Tall, but unhealthily thin.

Yet they are members of a team of men and women that continue to make sure that the dead zones are either loyal to or dead to the government. They hire random groups of people to spy on the distant communities. Some times they are successful; often the people never really make it back.

"It appears that our boy is inside, sir." They all speak at once. Their voices maintaining the same frequency and features as the others. Anyone in the room would not be able to tell differences between any of them.

"Our boy? Inside? Who is inside where?" The General is clueless. He doesn't remember ever ordering anyone to go anywhere. Nor was he aware of any such commands going out from his colleagues. "Explain yourselves. It's not the same one we were supposed to bring in."

They stand silently, in front of the General, as if to be either communicating with each other through telepathy or waiting for seats to magically appear behind themselves so that they can sit. They wait. Not one of them looks to either side. They continue to stare through the man in front of them expecting him to make the first move.

Maybe asking them to explain was too much. The General sits erect and stern behind his desk. Their gaze is making him feel a bit uneasy. It isn't often that an inferior subject can stare him down. Yet, these men were doing fairly well at making him want to divert his attention to something other than the three of them them. Anything...

After what seems like an eternity, the man on the far left begins to speak and the other two men take a step back from the wall they were forming in front of his desk. "Our boy is the kid that had been found responsible for the death of all those innocent people, in the Port City, Citru, on the East coast, over 10 months ago. The one that you had been chasing since the old cabin in Madaggan's old home town."

The man is direct and speaks firmly. "You do realize that you almost blew everything for us. How are we supposed to do our jobs when we have some other figure intercepting our mission? Fortunately, some kids picked up on what you left behind."

"Okay, I remember that kid. He took out the entire 76th block of that town." He pulls a hologram chip out of his desk and inserts it into the right slot on his clear frame. "As for us interfering with what you're trying to accomplish... There isn't anything in these orders which mentions what you are trying to do. I received orders directly from the President himself."

"Not to forget, the kid also completely obliterated 40% of our communication network. He took out the block, which possesses a majority of our programming stations. Many of which we were depending upon to locate 1,000's of unknown operational dead zones. The orders, including our mission, could have been lost in the network. That is of course, considering the fact that we still aren't currently running anywhere near our capacity."

"Yeah?" System failure can't be blamed here. Failure to communicate is the problem. The General knows that these guys usually operate under the radar with utmost secrecy. It's when too many people are trying to do the same thing that problems begin to appear. Unfortunately, it just happens to be that this time they are both attempting to accomplish the same thing.

"We planted a bug into that boy and sent him into a nearby sector. We practically made it so that the damn kid could waltz out of the place and wander directly into one of the zones we intended to invade. When you ordered the deployment of the Stalkers, you almost ruined our procedure.

Because of this, the Commander will be getting with you. You practically walked right over our ground operation and damn near prevented us from being able to follow him. Good thing we sent the bug in the kid. You have no idea what you could have done." The man still holds his posture and demanding voice.

"So, why have you come to me? What can I possibly do to help your section of the military?"

"Now…" He sucks in a deep breath. "We need you to do something for us and we hope you will cooperate. Should you choose not to aid us, we will simply go around you and do it without your assistance." He spins on his heals with his coat tail flailing behind.

"So, what do you need from me? I just lost six of my best transports."

One of the other two men steps forward. The first leaves the room. "Now, General, we need you to launch an attack on the very sector which took out your ships. Our boy is underground and your men need to seek out and destroy him and anyone who gets in your way. We are no longer concerned with keeping him alive."

He steps forward and sets the underground map onto the desktop and leaves a hologram chip. "They've taken shelter in an old underground bunker built in the 20th century." He pauses long enough to allow the General to give some sort of a response.

"You guys want me to send more men in there?" He shakes his head in disbelief. "You must be out of your mind. Why would I risk the lives of even more men so that you guys can wipe out one guy?"

"As we've already stated, asking for your help is merely courtesy, but we can do it all without any assistance." He nods and leaves the room as quickly as his associate.

The third man comes forward. "You have a decision to make. We will only wait for a few moments before going after the tracer." He stands stiff and stern as he has been the entire time he had been waiting to speak.

Why hadn't he known about this?

"I might add that if you choose not to do this, we will be using your troops anyhow. You won't be able to stop them once we get in. You must understand we are not going for just one person. We plan to kill them all."

"What!? How can you control my units without my authority?" Killing them isn't a problem. He has spent his entire life working up to this position. It was outrageous to even consider losing control of his troops to these people.

"There is only one way to do this. The Big Guy is on our side on this one." He pulls a paper out of his inside pocket. "This is the official notice that the President's power is supporting us and is willing to allow us to step over you. If you decide to get in our way, you will be joining those already inhabiting the darkness."

"You can't be serious! Honestly! You went to him before coming to me?! You haven't even given me a shot! Am I really that hard to work with?"

"We knew it wouldn't be easy."

How could they do this? How could they go above him and affect his job like this? Convincing the President wouldn't be hard. Was he willing to lose his position over this?

"Have you reached a decision?"

"I don't have a choice. I'll send them out now."

Meanwhile in the chambers of the mountains something has been discovered.

"Ron, the kid has a tracer!"

"We have to break it!"

In any area outside of the direct eye of the government, tracers are bad news. Tracers mean that They are on Their way. This also means that the zoners have been put in danger and now they have to move quickly. They have to get as far away from this spot as possible. Soon. Maybe, minutes from now. Possibly, it will happen hours later. There will be hundreds of people combing through these tunnels to unearth and then extinguish life. Unfortunately, this means trouble. They won't be coming just for the kid. They've planted it so that they could find those who they cannot control. Find and destroy...

Ron and Jerry respond by sounding an alarm, which only goes off behind the ears of those people who have gained citizenship of the colony. The people, sleeping under Cheetah's starlit sky, instantly prop themselves up and out of their cots. They stuff their beds so that it appears to look as if they are still asleep. This will either slow down the predator or prove to be a worthless strategy. Each member of the society grabs what little belongings they possess and uniformly headout of the immense space and on to their next home. Wherever that may be. This has become an all too common event. They are used to being on the run and defending themselves against whatever may be biting at their heels. Always ready, always moving. These people understand that this is what they have to do in order to remain independent. They know and have faith in the fact that they will, one day, be in the middle of an uprising fostered by the strengths of all the dead zones. All of them will eventually come together, march on the Capital, and knock down the system in order to rebuild it the way it should be.

J's body is the only life left behind. Right now he is a danger to them all. Before he can go any further, there has to be some changes. He carries the tracer and very few

148

people are willing to stay back and be caught by the retrievers. Those, who stay behind, will be held responsible for removing and destroying it. Even though they have to leave him behind, his time will soon come and his destiny soon fulfilled. It isn't often that the offspring of a seed comes back to the zones. For some reason, this one did. Whether or not he was aware of it, he was one of them. J's family had left the zones and infiltrated the city near the beginning of their creation almost 50 years ago.

Almost as soon as the cave had been emptied, a pack of people hurry to J's bed, put him into a deeper sleep with sleeping gas, start pumping morphine through his system, and begin the removal procedure. They know where to look and how to remove it. This isn't the first time they have had to do this. While he had been sleeping, the tracer had been located by Jerry's scan. Unfortunately, the morning's chaos made it so that he was unable to make it through the initial scan. He would never have been allowed this deep if they had known he was carrying the tracer.

This wouldn't take long. The government, Big Brother, always puts them in the same spot on either leg. They usually plant them on the inside of the bone of the carrier. That way they can't feel the device under their skin and easily remove it with a blade. Fortunately, they were able to do this without any pain to the mole and just a little discomfort and temporary nausea.

Quickly, they open him up, cut away the bone, and pull the tracer out of its place. J wakes, but not entirely before they put him back to sleep. They seal him up and use a laser to mend the wounds and make any scars virtually impossible to see. Then, without a moment's hesitation, they are gone.

XV

J can see masses of people are moving through the dimly lit caverns. He can't understand why they aren't moving faster. Don't they realize they are being followed? They are in danger. "Go!" J tries to urge them on, but they seem oblivious to his command. He gazes down upon them – young, old, men, and women. He can envision their innocent faces contorting with fear and panic as their yet unseen enemies surround them. "Move! They are coming!" J pleads with them, but to no avail.

The vision subsides, leaving J feeling on edge and uneasy. As his mind settles back into his own time and place, worry floods through every inch of his body. He bolts up from his cot, eyeing the floor beneath him.

"Go! We need to move!" He can feel something coming for him. A low rumble can be felt through the floor.

J grabs the girl who calls herself Cheetah, and runs towards Scott. With his other hand, he snatches a flashlight off of one of the cots, as he passes it, and turns it on. "Turn around! Get out of here!"

As he nears the hole in the wall, the floor beneath his cot gives way and everything within its mass is engulfed by the newly formed cavity. The cave is rocking so ferociously that the ceiling is feeding stones to the ground. Dust begins to rise from the center of the room.

Suddenly an enormous machine crawls out of the floor. It looks like a giant tank with a drill bit attached to its front end. The tracks are in two sets on each side. Each set rotating in opposite directions so that the machine is capable of flipping itself and moving in the same direction without damaging its body. When the monster had completely

150

submerged from the rocky depths, the drill stops spinning and it drops open to the stone floor.

J is still running, pulling Cheetah, and trying to convince Scott to move. They are almost through the exit. Scott still hasn't moved. No budge... Nothing... J yells, "Come on! Move your ass!" Nothing...

Scott stares in awe. The machine breaks through the ground and crashes into what has been his home for the past few months. An uninvited guest is now resting where he sleeps.

When the hatch opens, a series of red beams launch themselves through the air. They swarm the atmosphere like bees looking for a new hive to protect their queen.

J and Cheetah round the corner. They are safe. At the least they are temporarily safe. Yet, they continue to run. Fear of what is coming forces J to continue pushing on, his hand still wrapped securely around Cheetah's arm.

"I can run on my own!" Cheetah had been trying to pry loose of J's grip since he had grabbed her wrist. He wasn't registering her pleas. "It's a lot easier for us both to run if you just let go of me!" He let go. The thought of running back and rescuing Scott flickers in her mind, but she remembers that it is better that one escapes instead of none. If she goes back, she is certain to meet death.

It was like a programmed response. He is supposed to run. Everyone should be running. We can't defeat the system yet. They are far too strong. "Did you see that?"

"Yeah, what was it?"

Behind them, an explosion of shrapnel bounces off the passage walls. Surprisingly none of it rips through any of the stones. Whatever came out of that machine is now attacking the room it is in. A robotic monster erupts from the cloud of dust. Bullets now shower the room. Anything moving is now, or will soon be, dead. Scott isn't an exception.

Scott's body comes to a short rest on the stone walls of the cave and he falls to the floor, a lifeless mass. A long metallic arm flings from the monster and hovers over the body looking for any sign of life. Waiting for movement, it would destroy even the simplest flea jumping from the skin.

"Keep running!" J had let go of Cheetah, but he wanted her in front of him. They both knew the fate they would be forced to endure if they were captured. Now that they have seen the onslaught of the beast in the other room, they both know they don't want to be around when it comes through the wall. They are both running as fast as they can. They weave from one tunnel into another. Each path is shooting them in a different direction. Some climbing and others are falling. With only a flashlight to guide them through the darkness, it is amazing how quickly they adjust to new paths. Cheetah seems to know where to go. She leads and J follows.

Occasionally, J would shout to her not to go this way or that. Somehow, he could sense that they were being surrounded. J could sense other adversaries joining in the chase. He did not know whether this new prophetic ability was to be a blessing or a curse.

They dart through the passageways, running continuously on her lead and his instinct. For a second, he thought of Angel. He hoped that the girl had not met the same fate as Scott. He didn't even get a chance to really know these people, and already they are being cut out of the pages of his life.

J can feel his legs running, but he is no longer in control. He can feel his feet pounding the earth beneath him, but the dim outline of the tunnels fades away as he sees a group of people. They seem to be the same people he watched with such foreboding moments earlier. He remembered pleading with them to quicken their pace. Now they appear to be resting. He can see them, tired, waiting to rebuild strength to move on. They aren't in plain view of his eyes. So, he can't tell if they really exist or if they are just a part of his imagination. A part of what he is seeing.

J can feel that they are moments away from an aggressive onslaught. These troops will be invisible to the weary travelers, yet J can miraculously see them approaching. "They need to run!" He gasps through heavy breathing feeling his heart trying to leap out of his chest.

"Who?" Cheetah hoarsely questions J's words as she continues running.

"The people... They're still in harm's way. Soon..."

"Harm's way? What are you talking about? I know who you are and what everybody believes you will do for us, but you are beginning to scare me." She stops running, turns around, puts her hands on J's chest to stop him, and bends over with her hands on her knees to catch her breath. She isn't quite sure if she is going to hurl or if she needs a fresh breath of air.

"You shouldn't bend over. You'll get cramps."

"I can take care of myself." She looks him in the eyes. "Where are these people, kid?"

"I think I'm seeing things." He isn't sure if he should say anything about it. "I don't know how or why or what is even happening." Nothing like these visions has ever happened before.

"Sometimes people say we won't have to anymore."

"See things?"

"Yeah."

"What?"

"We can all see. Someday we won't have to any-more."

"What do you mean, 'we can see things'?"

"Nobody can really explain it. It's not like it always happens or we can just do it whenever we want. Our will doesn't control such an honor. It kinda seems like only one person can see it. Most of the time we don't know who is seeing what or when they've seen it. Even though we are asked not to tell, we often do when it is good or bad. Some keep it to themselves. That seems to be the most dangerous because they know something that can break us free." She pauses. Cheetah looks at the ground, smiles, and looks back at J. "This is how we found out about you."

"Are they always in the future or can you see what has already happened?" J hasn't seen anything that he could remember from the past, yet. Curiosity strikes him. As he speaks, he is watching the troops close in around the huddle of runaways. "This is awful. They are being surrounded."

"You can't do anything about it, ya know."

"Why not? People are going to die." He walks to the wall in front of him. "Are you ready to run again?" Troops walk closer to their prey. It is too late. Without showing themselves, they sweep the room. Without touching anyone, they pass through the crowd. Their number may have been a third of the refugees, but they were holding Spitters. With the amount of electricity that can fly from the Spitters, their smaller numbers wouldn't matter.

When they have finally covered the entire area, they stand still and motionless. They wait. Watching for their prey's next move, or waiting for some one else to show. Then, simultaneously, the troops place the Spitters at their hips and spray massive waves of energy into the crowd.

"What?" Cheetah is watching J. She knows he is seeing something new.

154

"They're gonna die, ya know." J crumples slightly towards the floor.

"Who?"

"Them." J points at the wall as if Cheetah can see what he is looking at. "They're being murdered."

She remains silent. No words could explain what is going through her mind. The visions are always right. What is seen can never be changed. It always happens. It has to. No one can prevent it. Not all were relatives. Yet, they were family in the sense that she was extremely close to them and they were all she had known for the past 10 years. Now, her family is gone.

A shock of pain bolts through J's body. He hunches over, holding his head with his hands. It felt as if his brain would begin to ooze from his skull through his ears. Another vision... more like a plunge of thoughts plowing through the nerves in his brain. He saw nothing. The word "run" continues to pelt him. He makes an attempt to yell out the word. He can say nothing.

The pain subsides and he is at least able to grab Cheetah's arm and start running again.

Cheetah complies with this physical command and resumes pulling J through the maze. J's brain is being swamped by whatever it is that wants him to flee. He is hard to pull and not an easy partner to run away with.

"Keep moving! He's somewhere within these walls! We won't allow him to skip out on us this time!" Jones is leading his group of cloaked men through the caves in search of J.

To the naked eye, none of the soldiers can be seen, nor would they be able to see each other. They communicate and see each other through a root cap and eye contacts.

Root caps are placed on top of a tooth in the mouth. These allow each person to talk with and listen to each member of the flock through thought. They have been specially designed so that the men do not have to say a word. The cap receives and transmits brain waves so that they can remain in stealth.

The contacts are smooth, a mixture of silver and gold, and implanted into the soldier's right eye. These allow the soldiers to see another cloaked comrade. This eye is designed so that they can be switched for different missions. Each eye carries special abilities for different situations.

In order for the troops to remain invisible, there has to be a programmer involved. The programmer is responsible for triggering the millions of molecular devices involved in the mission. If the programmer misses any reaction, from the messages being sent by the suit, then the cloak is no longer effective and the suits no longer operational.

Jones' troops flood through a room where bodies are huddled, dead, in the middle of the floor, and on to the next few passageways. Every time a fork comes up, the men split and divide themselves so they can cover more area in less time. The object is not to overwhelm by numbers, but to overcome by surprise. Their technology is doing specifically what it is expected to do. Allowing them to accomplish a majority of work with minimal effort.

Each passage offers them new possibilities. All of these men know that they are here to retrieve one person and eliminate the rest who are unlucky enough to get in the way. Even if they aren't directly preventing them from getting anywhere, these people have abandoned society and deserve death.

Deeper into the darkness guided only by their right eye and root caps, none know precisely where they are, where they have been, or where they will come out.

Unfortunately, these eyes do not allow them to see through the thickness of the walls. When the mission is complete, they will link back with the programmer and he will tell them the way out. Because he has been able to trace their every step, he has been drawing out a map from the paths they have taken. This will help if they ever have to come back here again.

The two come upon the end of a passage. Only using one flashlight between the two of them, J can see water running at the edge of the path. He shines the light in all directions. Darkness engulfs the rays of yellow.

"We jump in here, J." Cheetah is telling him what they have to do next in order to escape. She knows most of these tunnels like the back of her hand. There is no other way than through this stream.

"Really?" He expected the water would be ice cold, the journey would be long enough to freeze the two of them to death, and the ridged stones beneath the water dangerous enough to rip them open.

"Yes." She assured him.

"Won't we die of pneumonia or some other disease?" He stares at the water. "Isn't there another way?"

"There is no other way and you won't catch pneumonia. The water is fed by a hot spring. The stream is only 3 ½ feet deep and isn't pushing too hard. Fifteen feet ahead of us is a wall. The water streams under it."

"I'm not much of a swimmer." J barely feels comfortable spending time in a wading pool surrounded by people who could pull him above the surface if he were to go under. Something about not being able to see through to the bottom of this stream makes him feel even less at ease. "In fact, I don't really like water."

"It's either this or we go back and face whatever is waiting for us on those paths. There aren't many that will be able to follow us this far. I think I am now the only one alive who knows how to even get to this spring." She steps into the water and holds out a hand. "If I knew about another way out, I would have taken us that way. They'll be waiting for us at any of the other exits because they are the most obvious. Besides, the most dangerous thing you'll find in this water is the cavefish. I don't even think they have teeth."

J isn't exactly comforted. He still isn't sure why he is even here. It's all moving so fast. Does he keep running? Or, does he give in and go back? Only a crazy man would go back knowing that he is about to face whatever it was that cut down Scott. He throws his arm out in front, not really wanting to step foot in the water. "I guess fish aren't too bad."

"Come on."

They wade through the cold water. It's slight chill penetrating through their clothes. The spring warms the water just enough so that they aren't shivering uncontrollably. J finds himself remembering a freezing rain and a run through the woods.

For J, the fear of water is the only thing numbing him. Even with a flashlight that can clearly shine through to the floor of the pool he is standing in, he still isn't free of childhood fears of flesh eating fish lurking somewhere in the water. They say, "a grown man can drown in a spoonful of water." J could drown here. He could die soon. Something down there could brush his leg; he would freak out, go under, and drown. Would the girl pull him back up? Is it possible that she is with them and that she would shove him further down and hold him there?

Maybe some of the fish are cave piranha. Hunger for flesh will drive them to attack. When he goes down, they will strike and bite at his face. Cheetah would run away and let them feed on him. His flesh is definitely no match for the greatness of the sharp piranha teeth. Every few feet he slips his foot forward a few inches to check for some drop off where the bloody fish might be waiting for him.

Even though he resisted, Cheetah continued to yank on his arm and pull him through the water. He felt like dead weight on a slippery surface. Every other step, he was resisting and she would have to pull harder. She began wondering if the kid even wanted to escape. Kick him in the shin and pull him harder. Would he even budge a few inches further?

Miraculously, they arrived at the wall at the end of the pool. A slight current moves toward this side of the clear blue water. Darkness lurks just beyond that wall and J can feel it. No piranhas were tearing at his flesh so far. The only real threats are a bunch of moist sand and hard rock beneath his feet, along with a lot of water and constant worries.

"This is where we go under. We will only be under for a few seconds. Then, we come up in another small pool."

"I knew you were going to say that."

"You have to be more willing though. I can't drag you through like I did to get you here."

J takes a deep breath and looks down through the water. "Now or never." I'm gonna die!

She smiles. Looking at him, she can see he is fighting not to break down from fear.

I'm gonna die!

They go under. Darkness overwhelms them, but J manages to keep a firm hold on Cheetah. He counts the seconds as they go by. Even though she was right and they were literally under for just a few seconds, he is shaking when they come out of the water. Even though you couldn't tell because of his drenched clothes, he was sweating.

They surface under a low ceiling into an air pocket. Cheetah leads him out of the pool and into a narrow pathway. The walls of the path are waist high. They have to turn sideways in order to slide through. The walls are smooth and worn from unknown corrosion. J wonders how many others have come this way before him. Maybe the corrosion is a part of the bodies that have also rubbed their way through this path. Maybe, some of the zoners have already made it through here.

As they follow the steep incline, light ahead of them begins to strengthen out visibility. It isn't bright like that coming from the sun or the full moon on a cloudless night. The light is dim and pulsing like a rotating lighthouse lamp. As they come closer to the throbbing light, they can feel a pulsing vibration passing through the stone into their bodies.

J is glad to see that there may be more people ahead. Yet, he hopes Cheetah knows where she is going and isn't leading them into some sort of trap. She eagerly presses forward. She isn't showing any sign of trouble or unfamiliarity.

"We're almost there. Up ahead is another one of our units." She reaches out to her right side and pulls a stone back. A red light blinks next to a button. "This will make it so that no one can find the stream."

"Unit? What are you talking about?"

"We're some of the few who have survived." She stops, comes face to face with J, and grins. "You still don't get it do you? They've kept you in the dark the whole time haven't they?"

"What's there to get? The zones are areas where people are not supposed to exist. You hold the key to what happened to us during Madaggan's War. The zones are not in known connection with the majority of the world." He pauses, looks at one of the dusty walls, and draws a circle with his finger. He marks an x inside this circle, creates some curvy lines and a few more x's, and by the time he is finished, a flat globe of the world is present. "Of course, not all technology was taken away after Madaggan's War. We still have a sophisticated system. Most of the satellites and overseas communicators were taken out. My grandfather was a part of your group. The way he figured it, there are hundreds of thousands of people out there who are doing exactly what your group is trying to do." He points at the first x he had marked. "Your group was here. The rest of the x's represent the pockets of resistance which my grandfather knew about."

"He was a legend, kid." She rubs out the map. "A legend that would have never left evidence of our existence."

"You know him?"

"Everyone knows him. He was one of the few around when Madaggan's War began." She tugs on J's arm and begins walking again.

The resistance has existed since the war. When the people accidentally found out about Madaggan's plans to launch the nukes, they knew they would be in trouble. This led them to find cover and hoard supplies that they thought necessary for survival. Many of these people were able to escape and take refuge in remote areas.

J's grandfather was a militant who fought for Madaggan. As Chief Engineer, he was responsible for building some of the evacuation chambers. Needless to say, he knew what was happening. Because of the heads up, he saved the lives of his hometown friends by plotting where most of the bombs were most likely to hit. Then, he told them where to go or how to build their own shelters to stay alive.

His existence saved the extinction of millions. One of his only regrets had been that he couldn't save everyone.

XVI

Emerging from the wall, it slides closed behind them. They aren't outside, nor are they in a cave of passages anymore. A large space opens up before them. There are a few machines in different parts of this building. Despite the hum of these machines and the handful of people walking from one to the other, this might have easily been an abandoned complex. There are no windows, yet the facility is well lit by a natural light, which appears to be running the length of the facility.

J can't see exactly what the workers are doing or exactly what the purposes of the machines are. He is just thankful to be out of harms way. She has led him this far. All of the running is temporarily over. The water is back behind the walls and far away. The beast, from the other side, doesn't appear to be a threat anymore.

Two men appear from a door to the right. Cheetah walks towards them and opens her arms. A few words are exchanged between the three. She hugs them both and brings them back to J.

He feels uncomfortable. Once again he is being introduced to strangers in another unfamiliar place. At least he knows some one is looking out for him. So far, that is. Cheetah stands between the strangers, smiles, and introduces them.

"J, this here is Droi." She points to the darker man to her left. He looks as if he has spent many days of lying in the sun and working on his complexion. He wears the same pin striped navy blue jacket and pants as the other guy, but he seems to be uncomfortably fit at the seams. His hair has been bleached blonde. Even though it draped slightly over his ears, J could see the dark roots working through the yellow. His face is bony and narrow, unlike the rest of his body. It didn't seem to fit his weight. He wore a platinum grey band on his wrist. This could have been anything from a watch to a glasscutter. J wouldn't be surprised, with what he has seen in the past few days, if the guy set it down on the ground and it blew up into a compact airplane. J's grandfather had a few of these little gadget type watches.

J nods and sticks out his hand to greet Droi. He nods back. He didn't respond the way J expected.

"This is Troy." She points to the other man and he sticks his hand out right away.

"You'll have to forgive my partner. He's not much of a talker. Rarely ever responds to his own flatulence." Troy pumps his hand vigorously. "So, you're the kid?" He looks at J, rubs his chin, and traces him from head to foot. "How'd you make it all this way? We figured you for dead."

"Wasn't I supposed to?"

"Maybe. Who really knows? Do you think you're the only one that they have said would help them in their movement? Nobody ever knows which one of you will actually make it. They had a tracer on you. You're pretty lucky to be alive. Thank God for Cheetah." He rubs his neck. "They had one on me before." He lifts up his left pant leg to show a four-inch long scar. "They were chasing me. I found out I had it because it burned whenever they got close. I cut it out with a thin piece of metal found in some rubble."

Droi grunts.

J jumps not knowing what to expect from him.

"We need to keep moving guys." Cheetah starts walking across the floor towards the men in the white trench coats. "This kid is hot stuff. The other guys want him almost as bad as we do."

"They're waiting." Droi follows her.

"Who?"

"They are!" Troy points. There isn't anybody new in the area. The same workers, machines, and empty space still fill the space they had been before. "We never know exactly who. We just know when and where. That's all we're told. A different messenger comes every so often. I get a new partner and we move on." Troy and J follow.

"Where are we going?"

"We're going to end it all. We won't let a minor set back ruin the entire revolution. It must go on. Soon, we won't have to run anymore."

"Why do I need to go? What do you want with me?"

"I feel you already know these things. You are the one who is going to end it all for us. It's in your blood to do so. Kind of like your destiny set in stone." He sighs. "Of course, you understand we have to complete the delivery before the dream can become a reality."

Cheetah and Droi disappear.

Outside a Warf hovers waiting for its riders. The Warf is a transport hovercraft that can carry up to 10 passengers. It is rather slow when compared to most crafts of its size, but it is heavily armored. If ever there would be trouble, a person would feel safer in this vehicle than in any other.

The sky is beginning to fade to darkness. The moon is orange and sitting just above the tree line in the East. It lights up much of the sky and drowns out the existence of any early stars.

Cheetah and Droi are already sitting in the Warf. J inhales deeply. It has only been a day since he has been in fresh air. So much seems to have passed by. What new task lies ahead? They are still chasing. How is it possible for him to get away when he is sitting in their back yard?

Troy climbs into the Warf and J follows.

Droi is fidgeting with some gadgets at the front of the vehicle. Cheetah sits comfortably in one of the air filled synthetic leather seats. Troy offers a drink to J and gulps down his own. The craft begins to humm and rise from its resting spot.

"This is the inside of a Warf, huh? J takes in his new surroundings. The immense armor on the outside makes the vehicle seem like it would be cramped on the inside. Yet, there is a vast amount of space to move around in. "Never been in one before."

"Really?"

"Yeah." Not many are ever in a government built vehicle. Especially if you don't work for them.

"This is a company issued vehicle. They had it specially built for our line of work and the boss's services. We've got everything in here. The hologram rises from the center of the floor. The seats fold down and we can play craps or just try our luck with the slots. This is like our own little party on the road. Of course, you probably already know about the armor."

"Yeah, best armor of any vehicle in any class. Even better than some of the highest military vehicles."

"We upgraded it. It is now better than any defense vehicle in any class. It can also put up a good battle with some assault vehicles. This is so, primarily, because of its defenses. We've equipped some blasters that drop from the floor. If that's not enough, we've put some 70mm shells in the back of this beast. When stationary and by herself, we can call her into service and she'll rip down anything we want."

"Why all this juice? More importantly, how did you get all of this power without the government finding out?" It's not possible that the government would allow anybody to just build one of these without their permission.

"The boss is an important man. Not only to us, but also to the system itself. He had it built. We just work for him. We think he works for the opposition and hires us to keep things in balance."

"He runs the whole operation, J." Cheetah slouches back in her seat. "He controls it all from top to bottom. Remember the guy you saw on the hologram back in the cave? We work for him and he works for us."

"This baby," Troy kept going, "is the cream of the crop. No one has anything like this." He sips more of his beverage.

"Who is the boss?"

Silence... Troy swallows, Cheetah puts her hands behind her neck and leans back even further, and Droi continues to focus on maneuvering the Warf with the control panel to the front of the vehicle. No one answers. Eye contact suddenly disappears. Silence...

J clears his throat and begins to say something.

"No one knows his name." Droi spoke.

J was set back, not by what had been said, but by the fact that he had actually said words. Even though his knowledge of Droi is limited, it has been made clear that he is not a conversationalist.

J waits for Droi to elaborate.

Nothing... Silence broken only by the light purr of the moving craft. After a few seconds, feeling like minutes, J shakes himself back into reality.

"No one knows his name?"

"Yeah. That's what I said." Droi didn't look up. "I'm the only one to have ever seen him in person... kind of."

"Kind of?"

The other two shift their weight where they are sitting.

"What do you mean, kind of? You all work for and trust a man who you don't even know and haven't ever seen?"

"Almost home." Droi turns to another panel and the windows shade themselves down to pitch black. The question goes unanswered.

"We're almost home, kid." Troy pulls a flat oval from the front of his suit, touches J with it, and watches as J slowly loses consciousness. He never saw it coming and he couldn't fight it off. Sleep follows a simple prick on the neck.

XVII

"Do you think the operation was a success?"

"Yes, sir."

"Tell me, Pecker. How was it a success?"

"We eliminated most of the opposition, sir." Pecker shifts in his seat. "We were able to capture men and women for questioning. Their information should lead us to what you are looking for."

"Did you get him?" Barely anyone had actually been spared. Besides, retrieving J is the only thing he cares about. Hopefully, they didn't kill him when they went on their rampage.

"No, sir."

"You didn't get him! He's the only reason we went there! I hope you weren't thinking that I am going to allow this failure to pass!" Cane walks around from behind his desk, and towers over Pecker. "This is unacceptable! Find him now! Or, you can find yourself a new job!"

"We're already on it, sir. We've planted a virus." Pecker inches his seat away from where the General is standing. "He's in the city, sir."

"A virus? Who do we have?"

"You don't know this man, sir." Pecker offers the folder, sitting on his lap, to Cane. "We've offered him his freedom for this job. We convinced him that anything is better than sitting in a cell wishing you were already dead."

"Who is this guy?" A chance has resurfaced...

"He's a former inmate. Name is Dave Ingham. Used to hack our systems. We won't have to worry about him doing it again though. Upon arrival and delivery he will breathe no more."

"You realize the President wants this kid alive? He holds some sort of value towards him. If anything happens to him, you will pay for it. I won't take the fall for this one."

Pecker nods. "We know what he wants and we know why he wants him. I will personally see to it that this boy is brought home."

Cane backs away from Pecker and turns to look out his office window. Throughout the city he can see people wandering through the streets, either on their way home from work or on to fulfill the economic freedom of entertainment. "We've come so far. Do you understand this? We can't afford to face the war ahead of us. The world cannot afford the aftermath of it. Madaggan did not do what he did so that we could end up like this."

"Sir, we can do this. It's just one person."

"Just one person?" He turns and locks eyes with Pecker. "This one person could be a part of the prophecy!" He steps over to the projector near the window. He pushes the button on. The country motto begins to play. "This makes us who we are. That little song, that you hear everyday, when you wake up. Think about what it means. Think about the people who had to suffer so that our families could become a part of the new federation of people."

Pecker begins to chant the words of the song as it fills the air around them.

Here comes the Big One

We gathered all of our guns

Now to take away what's wrong

The Sons of Liberty have been here too long

Madaggan's Federation will aid us

They will shelter us

Let them rise into the days to come

Shut down the enemy wherever they are from

Welcome a new generation

Welcome Madaggan's Federation

"We have to uphold the values of the Federation. That kid represents those who do not believe in our values." He pauses, slides a panel of the wall to his left, and a hole appears. An oval shaped arrangement of buttons light up. "You want something?" He glides his hand over a few buttons. Within a few seconds an ice-cold beverage appears.

"No thanks." He pulls a briefcase from the floor and opens it onto Cane's desk. "Besides being a capable hacker, Ingham also specializes in mole operations. He is good enough to have been able to infiltrate our own military bases and cut into our communication from within."

"Can he do the job?"

"If he doesn't... it will be far too easy to find him. Failure will not be tolerated."

"We're here." Droi lowers the Warf and it humms off. "Let's go." He kicks Cheetah's chair and wakes her from her power nap.

Troy opens the hatch and steps out. "Hey, Droi, what is this place? We weren't supposed to head to the city."

Droi pulls a blaster from under his jacket and vaporizes Troy and Cheetah. "Don't move, kid."

Tired, from the drug he had been hit with earlier, he sits back in his seat. What else could he do? "What gives,

170

man?" Escape! Run! Die! What is this freak gonna do? If he budges, he is sure to be sharing space in the afterlife with the other two. That is, if he didn't feel so sluggish and actually wanted to make an attempt to jet.

"Boss wants to see you personally." Droi takes off his jacket and reveals a dark red symbol on his shirt. A square possesses a triangle and the initials DD. "Come on."

Droi grabs J. His grip is powerful. He feels like a little boy being held up by his father. His grip is strong enough to make the vessels in his hand involuntarily bulge through the skin. J spins his wrist and shockingly breaks Droi's grip. J instantly grabs his wrist and winces at the pain caused by Droi's grip. Droi instantly spins around and thrusts the tip of his blaster into J's face.

"They want you alive. Don't make me have to fail my objective." He presses the blaster into J's eye socket. "You're nothing but a fucking punk and a free ticket. You screw this up for me and I'll kill ya."

J throws his arms up and tries to back away. He hits his head on one of the guns sticking out from the Warf and is held there by the blaster. "I don't want any trouble. Why are you doing this?" Didn't see this coming. Can't believe this is happening.

"Shut up!" This is Droi's one shot. Deliver the kid and be forever free.

J doesn't move. He waits. Troy and Cheetah couldn't have known who this maniac really is. Cheetah wouldn't have led him into this, had she known it was coming. He says nothing else, wondering what is to become of him.

"Move on!" Droi pulls the blaster away, grabs his shoulder, and throws J away from the Warf. Now, instead of his face, Droi is trying to force the blaster through his neck. If he shoves any harder, he is sure to leave an ever-lasting scar to the front. "Don't be stupid, kid!"

J moves on. He walks quickly and smoothly as he is forced to do. The building in front of him has to be one of the largest in the city. Spotlights shooting up from the ground vaguely light it up. The walkway, from the Warf, is made of marble. It is a typical straight path with a triangle guiding it to the front door. It curves at some points and narrows in others where trees and shrubbery grow. The walk takes the two men across a bridge of ten feet hovering over a small stream. It appears to have been built some time in a distant past.

J can see that generations of families have controlled this structure at one time or another. Symbols of different companies have been sun burned onto the front of the building and into the marble on which he is walking. Presently, the initials DD show themselves boldly and stronger than all the rest.

As the two approach the main entrance, it raises and exposes a twenty-foot stained glass mural of a man holding a book in one hand and a map of the world in the other. This represents the belief that Madaggan was a wise, educated man, who knew what it would take to rule the world. His picture had him staring and looking off into an eastward direction.

"He had big plans. He was supposed to have known what we would need to survive." Droi shoves J into the glass, reaches to the right, and pulls a piece of glass away from the rest. Another slab of the mural swings open to let them in.

"Yeah, I know, he had plans to conquer the world and unify us all under one flag. He expected peace to reign from destruction." J grits his teeth, rubs his chest, and fades through the newly open doorway. "He wasn't successful."

"He was betrayed." Droi continues to push him forward. "People like you betrayed him. Your kind destroyed any chances we could have had of a world wide Utopia. We could have still been living in peace and not having to worry about the likes of your people."

"It would have never lasted." J takes in the long narrow hall. Not many doors exist on this path. It is long and narrow and looks to hold only one door at its end. "He didn't really want peace. If successful, he would have seen to the destruction of everyone who opposed his ideals."

Droi punches him in his back. "Keep walking, traitor!" He shoves the blaster in his mid section. "We've still got our plans. We'll have it our way."

Plans? What plans? At the end of all this, he will probably end up dead? Point gun. Shoot. Wow, now that's a plan. Even a thug like Droi has the ability to be more creative than that. What now? Biological death? Date with a doctor who is craving a bit of cutting? What plans?

J's knees give out and he falls to the floor. Droi scrapes him off the floor and forces him into the elevator where he falls to the carpet. The door shuts, a bell dings, and the back door opens.

XVIII

J falls forward as Droi attempts to pull him out of the elevator. He hits the hard wood floor beneath him. In front of them lay an elegant room and a piece of history. The person, who owns this place, has both a lot of money and a massive amount of power in the world. No normal citizen can afford the price of the wood in this room, let alone the furniture present. Most citizens are lucky just to see furniture made of real wood. Even a tree is a blessing to have. Even the park in front of grandfather's place, had only one tree in its middle.

In the middle of the room lay an Asian rug in beautiful bright colors. The patterns are simply words embroidered in Chinese lettering. He couldn't read it, but recognized it from World History. It's a piece that had been given to Madaggan when he first took office.

On the rug, sits a glass display of a world globe. Of all things to be held in a display case, why would anyone want to put the world here? What is so significant about this that it is on display in the center of a room? Perhaps a symbol of world domination.

Droi now has his foot pressing down on J's back so that it is impossible for him to move around and look closer at any of the treasures held within these walls.

The walls in this room are filled with murals made out of different types of wood. One mural has an eagle flying over the capital building with a globe in one claw and the American seal in the other. J knows this is to show that America had once been the dominant force in the world, pre Madaggan. Now, the people fight a bitter struggle with the former most powerful nation in the world. A simple twist of

174

fate. Changes of power are continuously repeated throughout history.

"Imagine that," J manages to mutter.

"What?"

J had almost forgotten that Droi had been shoving his foot through his spine. "I said, imagine that."

"Imagine what?" Droi relieves a bit of pressure so that J can respond.

"We used to be strong. We used to be feared by the rest of the world. No one could stop us. Do your plans have anything to do with making us that way again?"

"What cher point, kid?"

"Now, we fight ourselves. I think that history points out that a country divided cannot stand. Yet, we still fight with ourselves."

Droi picks J up. "This is where my job is finished. Good luck, kid." He steps back into the elevator. As the elevator closes, a wall drops down in its place.

J looks around the room and spends time admiring his newest atmosphere. It is awesome for a person, in this age to be standing in a room surrounded simply by things which common people have been denied. J's grandfather belonged to the last generation of people who were allowed to write on paper made from trees. They were the last to roam through the country freely, as tourists, and around the world. They were the last to celebrate the might and honor of this once flourishing country. Only sixty years... That war changed it all. Who would have ever believed that one man had so much power to change the future.

Standing in this room angered and elevated his hate for this country. Whomever lives here is experiencing life the way that all of America's people should be living. How is it right for the people to suffer and the system to thrive and protect its own way of life?

J walks across the room to a desk beyond the glass globe. On the desk lay a copy of the Constitution with its fifty amendments. The framers had great ideas. Too bad the Congress took advantage of their power in a time of conflict. During the war, the last five Amendments were framed into the Document. It practically threw out everything before them and restructured a new law for the country. They should have taken the Constitution away and started with a new sheet of paper. Before this, J had never seen an actual copy of this document. Schools are no longer allowed to discuss it. It would be set aside as something that only military students would see. The public is kept ignorant of its changes and the military is responsible for enforcing what the people do not know.

If the people had been able to vote on the Amendments, they would have never allowed them to have so much power. Representatives gave away the power of the citizens and allowed the President ultimate authority. Madaggan was an outstanding speaker. None of the voters would have allowed this. Had the country not been in a severe period of depression and desperate to get out, these additions would have never been made. Unfortunately, the powers of the President have been broken up and distributed to a mass of government officials who have manipulated the government to bend to their will.

After studying the paper, he turns left and walks over to a hologram display case. Every few seconds a model of a person would appear and spin above the table. Next to a few touch screen buttons, a list of directions are printed on how to use the machine. It is a holographic monument of the men and women that were a part of everything leading up to Madaggan's War.

He touches one of the buttons labeled victims. A list of names arranged themselves as new buttons on the screen.

"If you press one of the following names, you will hear a short biography of that person." The machine speaks to him and he waits. He scans the list. Not many of the names are familiar.

He touches one that reads McGregor Jones. A black man, dressed in a suit and tie, appears before his eyes. He looks like a worn man. His eyes are deeply set and his skin extremely weathered. Yet, he smiles. "McGregor Jones..." the computer reads his profile. "Killed by chemical warfare during the Great War. He... along with thousands of other Washington citizens never got to see the beauty that our country has become. Long live peace..." it stops and the man disappears.

The names on the screen shrink and narrow themselves. "These are your relatives who were affected by the war." The computer must have read his prints when he touched Jones' button. J recognizes some of the names. They are mostly his grandfather's brothers, sisters, and other people he can remember hearing mentioned by him.

J presses another button. "Hector J Mann. A former engineering specialist... he managed to become one of the few known men to make it through the war. He was lost for ten years when his helicopter crashed in West Virginia. Formerly classified as MIA, he appeared at one of our outreaching bases claiming to be an amnesiac. Recently, he was involved in a resistance movement against those who had helped him become a better person in society. As a result, he has been eliminated. This was truly a sad day in our past." The hologram shifts the man's appearance as it ages through his life description.

"Hector, huh? I never knew his real name."

Behind J, the wall opens. Two men enter and stare at J. He doesn't run or try to escape. There seems to be no where else to go and no reason to fight. Die now, or die later. If he tries to run they will definitely be able to prevent him from going too far. Who knows what kind of traps they have set up within the walls of this building?

They sit themselves down in a couple of chairs on the other side of the room. J watches. They signal for him to come over and join them. Cautiously, he finds his way over to them and sits in the only chair left. He glares at them as they stare back and wait for him to be seated.

"You know..." the older man begins. "You've been a menace to us. A real thorn in our sides." He turns to the other man. "Good job, Pecker. Your man did the job." He refocuses on J. "Who are you working for?"

"Who am I working for?" What kind of question is that? It's not like he chose to come here.

The ceiling above them opens up and the floor beneath begins to rise. As it rises, the ceilings above continue to disappear. Floor by floor they continue to rise in silence. The end of their short trip brings them to a glass room.

"It's a beautiful night out, J." The older man stands up and leaves his chair. The other man follows and motions for J to leave his seat also. As the two step off the platform, it begins to sink. J Scrambles from his seat and off the moving floor. "The trip down would have been much harder, kid."

"Why am I here? How do you know me?" J is becoming uneasy and wanting to move on. Desiring only to know what the point of all this is. Whatever they are going to do, they need to hurry up and do it.

Through the glass windows, stars and the bright shine of the full moon light up the sky. There hangs the occasional cloud, but nothing large enough to threaten the illumination of the moon.

The city is dimly lit up by a few house lights shouting through the darkness. Curfew is in effect. No one should be out at this time of night. Unless, of course, they are criminals. A rare siren blares in the distance. Yet, J recognizes its meaning. A routine violator, being brought in.

"You are here because we want you to be." Pecker speaks, pulls out a small square and starts plugging at it with an even smaller wand. "You could have been killed." He cracks a smile and laughs. "That is, if we wanted you dead." He continues to plug away at the device in his hand.

These men still aren't truly answering why J is here or even why they haven't already taken care of him. Eliminate the threat. Knock out the opposition. That is what they think he is, isn't it? Then why aren't they going along with what they teach? That is practically all we ever needed to know about Madaggan's War. If there is something in the path, move it out of the way. In this case, if they also believed J to be a part of the tool to destroy the system, then they had to do it, but they aren't motioning any immediate threat.

"By having me here, you won't stop the resistance from coming. Millions of them don't even know about me. They all seem to believe in something or someone different. Besides, you know as well as I do that they have the technology to do anything now. They have the capability to muster up more people than even your own government can." J is bluffing. He isn't sure if what he is saying is true. It just sounds like it needs to be said. Yet, he knows, from his grandfather's talks, that there are colonies of people spread out across the country. "When they start…"

"They won't be able to start, J. They will not rise!" The older man walks over to one of the near windows and pounds his fist on the ledge.

"Frustrated?" A smirk appears on J's face.

"What you don't understand is that you can't stop us! We run this country! Even as pathetic as it has been! For the people, by the people! What a joke." He pauses and looks out beyond the city. "Screw the people! Give them a chance to control themselves? All they ever did was complain. How is it that the minority was ever allowed to run this country through an organized 'vote'? Why allow ignorant fools to run what we control through a vote? As the government, the intelligent minority can finally be represented and controlling of the majority." He walks away from the window and over to an empty wall on the East side of the room.

"What is that supposed to mean?"

"You'll see." After prodding at a few stains on the wall, a few colors begin blipping where the stains were. In a few seconds, the entire wall is a topographical map of the United States. Areas of the map are solid oranges, reds, and blues. Other parts are simply shades of these three colors. The majority of the country is covered in black with occasional white bleeps.

"As you can see, this is a map of the wonderful nation we have been blessed to run. All of the orange areas are where we are on complete alert. The red areas represent zones where we are eliminating the opposition. The blue, and there is a lot of it, 90% of the inhabitants have been injected with a monitoring subject. Upon our command, the brain's chemicals will trigger a complete shut down. If not treated soon afterwards, they die. So... Now, I ask you, who is in control?"

"Why?" J gazes at the map. "How can our government want... or do this? Let them come back into society and you won't have to spend an eternity chasing them!"

"Easy." He turns and faces J. "We demand control. We need it! Those who resist... they die! Let them come back and we pick up where we left off. All they do is complain about everything. 'We want our rights. We want to vote. Legalize this. Legalize that.' They will never be satisfied!"

180

"What about the white lights spread out across the continent?" J can't help but express his curiosity.

"Those are the dead zones. The lights represent our lookout. We have someone everywhere. Never can be too safe." He chuckles. "Anyone out there can't be allowed to come back. We are keeping their existence as low as we can."

"You guys are sick, you know that? Killing people just because you don't want to play the true role of a government. That can't be right."

Pecker stands up, walks over to J, and shoves him down into a chair. "You are in no position to speak like that!" He bends down and gets into his face. "You are the one causing us trouble! You're not cooperating with the network!" Pecker begins shaking him. J crosses his arms in front of his face.

"Stop!" He brings his arms out and pushes Pecker back. Leaping from his chair, he shoves Pecker back again. "Why would I cooperate? I know nothing of what you are expecting from me! Everyone is feeding me with a bunch of bullshit! How could I possibly know what to do?" Pecker comes back at him with his arms outstretched. J moves to the side and throws him to the ground. "Just because you are a part of them, doesn't mean I am going to stand here and let you push me around!" J glares down at him. He kicks his leg adding to insult. "I'll voluntarily listen to whatever you have to say! I'll let you believe what you wish. But, there isn't any way I am going to let a worm, like you, push me around!"

Pecker crawls out of reach and stands up. He rubs a flush of blood from the corner of his mouth.

The older man intervenes and pulls J's attention back to the country map. "All right, kid, we get your point. We just need to know why you haven't been cooperating." He shoots a hard eye at Pecker for his foolish actions.

"I still don't understand. Why would I have to cooperate with you?"

"Owner owns."

"What?"

"Owner owns."

"It doesn't work, sir." Pecker speaks up. The password has been removed. Controlling J isn't an option.

"What doesn't work? Is this some sort of mind control junk?"

"Nothing."

"It's time, sir." Pecker points to the window and the city is under attack.

XIX

Under the camouflage of night, they move. Through the darkness, they stalk forth for independence. Independence or unification? Soon, these people will be fighting a battle that they are all supposed to believe in. All of this time has been used for preparation. If you ask any of them what they are fighting for, they will answer 'independence' or 'unification'. They will shout it and understand what it is supposed to be. As a unit, the goal is understood by all that are within it.

As individuals, each one has their own ideas of what they would like to do with the future. Only the future will unfold stories that none of them can predict. If this revolution succeeds, who will lead? How will they rule or be ruled? How will these things be determined?

Since the Great War, the dead zones have had to deal with the issue of reunification. Would they be willing to reunite with a country that doomed its own people? Those who have come before them and tried to do so have died instantly at the arms of the government. As wide spread as the arms can get, the government made every attempt possible to prevent the zones from joining with the rest of the world. When you look at an enemy who is this deranged, how can you let them live among you?

They were never warned. It all just happened. The bombs were dropped and all of their lives were changed. None of the brave people fighting the revolution can remember when the country was one, but they have heard stories of how everything had been different. These stories fed hope that someday, it would all be normal again. Fight for normality. Bring the country back to the way it used to be.

On the other side of the coin, they had to decide whether or not they would fight for their independence from a people who refuse to acknowledge their existence. When it was dropped, they were all presumed extinct. The possibility of life after Madaggan's War created frustration. They, who survived, did not want to be run by the same men who jeopardized their lives. Now, it is their turn to deal punishment for the way they have been treated.

The line between good and evil has become blurred. Over the course of 60 years, the zones have been able to infiltrate the system. Pledging a false loyalty allows them to mold into society undetected. Now, when it matters, it is up to these people to follow through with what they have been taught and trained to do. Because they have been planted in every sector of the government, the battle should only take one night.

The system has declared us dead and works fervently for us to be so. No one knows who we are or where we will come from. Only we know where all of the others are. We've been tossed out! Now, they will feel their mistake. We will make them feel it! Last night, they raided and wiped out an entire colony.

We fight on. We move now. To prolong this event, at hand, would allow more time for them to prepare. If they know we are coming, we are already doomed, but they have no idea that we are coming or when we will strike. We will come externally and internally. All of us should be on the move now!

This message and more is relayed out to the pockets of resistance that have answered the call for action. In a single movement, the entire country is invaded by small numbers of men and women from within the cities and practically every able person in the zones. A massive onslaught of explosives destroyed any, if not all policing and military centers known by the zones. Every united town running under the current government is feeling the wrath of the revolution. They are single-handedly victorious against a large force. They had to shut down the Big Guys. No more innocent massacres. No more brainwashing. No more repression of anger.

J stares in astonishment as the town suddenly bursts and crumbles under its own flames. Instantly, debris is flying and buildings are collapsing before his eyes. For a moment, he thought he too would fall as the structure in which he was standing rattled to the earth. Only a slight tremor pulses through its walls. Yet, around it, everything else appears to be gone.

Below, he can see people running through the streets. Some are fleeing to avoid death. Others are scavenging through the debris for whatever or whomever they can find. J wonders if any are rushing to the injured or dead for purposes other than to rob them. Medical response units should have been hitting the roads to care for the injured, but J knew that this would be limited to a rare unit. Not enough to make a dent in what has just taken place before his own eyes.

"If you want to defeat a person, take away his will to fight. Then take away his means of protection. If you can't control these things, hit him with everything you can."

– Madaggan

Though he cannot hear it, he imagines the sounds of suffering and crying for help that must be emanating through the city. He knew that Grandfather had always warned of this day. When it would come. Only those involved in the attack would know precisely when. Because of the curfew, millions would die. They knew this. Millions are now dead.

The old man and Pecker stand in silence. They seem to be both shocked at the same time. They, too, knew that this day was coming. They never knew when or where.

"Let it be the end of the enemy and the beginning of a new era. In this new era, may you find peace and justification for your cause." – Madaggan

The old man turns to J. "I guess they really didn't need you after all. You weren't who we thought you were." He pulls out a dagger and stabs J in the chest. Before J can react, it is done again and again. He continues to thrust the cold blade repeatedly until his arm is tired. J can only sit and look as his breath slowly escapes him and his energy dwindles.

He falls to the floor unable to do anything in his own defense. Pain... Warmth... Coldness... His eyes close... Breath no longer passes through his lips.

Without him, times move on

With him, nothing is getting done

We had to revolt

With a lightning like jolt

His sacrifice is what made this right

As we stole their lives throughout the night

Victory... Victory... Victory is ours... - Revolutionaries

Epilogue

J's manner of death goes unknown by the people and he is seen as a martyr who had been sent to help them in their mission. So do the lives of the others that were thought to be the Chosen One. Their disappearances give them more reason to believe that their existence was a necessary sacrifice for their cause. For their cause, the innocent have died.

The government was defeated with very little resistance. The sudden surprise caught them off guard. The years of planning and planting rebels inside the network, paid off when it was most vital. They knew their jobs and did exactly what was expected.

At the end of the war, the Revolutionaries (this is what history has named them) were finally able to come together as one. This is the last time any group meets representing the same cause. This day was supposed to set up the future of a country that they had hoped to save from destruction.

Instead of manhandling destiny and recreating a country that they could all agree to live in, they argued like toddlers. They couldn't come to an agreement on how the states would be run. Redrafting a Constitution turned out to be impossible. They saw eye – to – eye on one thing… Disagreement.

Because conflict ruled, the people decided to divide the country according to various theories of government. The people believing in one thing, went that way. People believing in another, molded into that given ideology.

They tried to go back to the old way, but they couldn't come to terms under which the country should be run. After eight years, they set the boundaries and drew up treaties outlining the space they would be given for the different factions of government. They drafted treaties to wars that were never fought and gave away that which was never lost.

This idea leaves many wondering if the revolution was a success or it merely opened the door to even harder times. People lived within the boundaries set up by the treaties. Multitudes of people never let go of the original revolutionary ideals. They never saw the revolution as finished. Now, they were presented with a new enemy and a new cause to which they were to dedicate their time.

What was the true purpose of the revolution? Break up a country? Set up a new system for failure? Or... Was it just another way for the people to show that they can never be satisfied? Change and dissatisfaction are the only constants.

Pockets of resistance still exist within these newly formed units. A hunger to control thrived in their minds. People still struggle, and the lot of many would still be forced to do what the few, in power, choose for them. Such is the greed of the government in every form and nation.

Independence was won.

"Was it worth the lives lost? Will the burdens of the past make the future easier? Is this the Independence you were expecting?" – C. Martin

"Society reigns in an era of Eternal Discontent." – T. Phillips